"I'm taking you ⟨ P9-CRK-599 **poacher shouted to Lex.**

"I'm going to walk out of here, and you're not going to stop me."

"No." Poppy's voice rose, calm and clear. "Set Danny down gently, drop your weapon and raise your hands now."

The poacher snorted, pulled the gun away from Danny's side and pointed it right between Poppy's eyes. "I thought we showed you we meant business," the poacher said. "But you wanted to learn the lesson the hard way."

Poppy let go of Stormy's collar. "Stormy! Protect Danny!"

Snarling, Stormy leaped...

ALASKA K-9 UNIT

Maggie K. Black is an award-winning journalist and romantic suspense author with an insatiable love of traveling the world. She has lived in the American South, Europe and the Middle East. She now makes her home in Canada with her history-teacher husband, their two beautiful girls and a small but mighty dog. Maggie enjoys connecting with her readers at maggiekblack.com.

Books by Maggie K. Black

Love Inspired Suspense

Alaska K-9 Unit
Wilderness Defender

Protected Identities
Christmas Witness Protection
Runaway Witness
Christmas Witness Conspiracy

True North Heroes
Undercover Holiday Fiancée
The Littlest Target
Rescuing His Secret Child
Cold Case Secrets

Amish Witness Protection
Amish Hideout

Military K-9 Unit
Standing Fast

Visit the Author Profile page at Harlequin.com for more titles.

WILDERNESS DEFENDER

MAGGIE K. BLACK

LOVE INSPIRED SUSPENSE
INSPIRATIONAL ROMANCE

Special thanks and acknowledgment are given to Maggie K. Black
for her contribution to the Alaska K-9 Unit miniseries.

LOVE INSPIRED® SUSPENSE
INSPIRATIONAL ROMANCE

Recycling programs
for this product may
not exist in your area.

ISBN-13: 978-1-335-72239-3

Wilderness Defender

Copyright © 2021 by Harlequin Books S.A.

This edition published by arrangement with Harlequin Books S.A.

For questions and comments about the quality of this book, please contact us
at CustomerService@Harlequin.com.

Love Inspired
22 Adelaide St. West, 40th Floor
Toronto, Ontario M5H 4E3, Canada
www.Harlequin.com

Printed in U.S.A.

And the Lord God said,
It is not good that man should be alone.
—Genesis 2:18

To all those who are trying to do it all
and all those stepping in to help others

ONE

Despite the bright blue of the May sky above, a chill cut through the Alaskan air that sent shivers of trepidation running down Trooper Poppy Walsh's spine. Her eyes scanned the empty windows of Glacier Bay National Park's remote cabins. The place was deserted, still awaiting the flocks of tourists who'd arrive in the coming weeks when things really kicked off for the season.

It was the unwelcomed guests who might've been squatting here as they illegally hunted defenseless bear cubs that she and her K-9 partner, Stormy, were here to sniff out. The body of a known poacher had been found shot dead and floating in the water by park troopers. Rumor among the locals was that his fellow poachers had turned on him after they captured a cub and that they were now hunting the park for the baby bear's sibling.

Poppy glanced around the towering spruce and made sure they were alone. Then she reached over and unclipped the Irish wolfhound from her leash. She ran her hand along Stormy's shaggy gray fur, feeling the dog's tension radiating through her fingers. Standing at almost three feet tall on all fours, with a friendly hound-dog face and a protective guardian nature, it took a lot to put the dog on edge. Did Stormy detect something? Or was she just reflecting Poppy's own uneasiness back to her like a mirror?

Poppy prayed and asked God to help her focus. If poachers were hiding out somewhere in the park, that could put tourists' lives in danger, as well as those of the baby animals they captured to sell on the black market. And yet, Poppy's nerves had been frayed ever since the small plane that had brought herself, fellow trooper Will Stryker and their K-9 partners here had taken off from Anchorage. As they'd circled the airstrip of the small town of Gustavus, and she'd looked down to see a scattering of houses give way to a port full of boats, towering trees, majestic glaciers and the roaring Pacific beyond, just one thought had filled her mind—this was where she and Lex Fielding were supposed to go on their honeymoon.

The park ranger had been the reason she'd finally given up her job at Kenai Fjords National Park to become a K-9 trooper. On the night he'd taken her face into his strong hands and asked her to be his wife, her former colleague had told Poppy the deep green of her eyes reminded him of the Glacier Bay's evergreens. He'd promised to bring her here. Just like he'd promised to marry her and to stand by her side for everything life threw at them. Instead, his fear of being anyone's husband or father had apparently wrenched them apart and he'd broken her heart, calling off the wedding just a week before the big day and leaving her with an invisible wound that still ached after all these years. For a moment, Lex's dark serious eyes and rare but generous smile hovered at the edges of her mind. Her chin rose as she shoved thoughts of him away. She was proud of the fact she'd managed to maintain her cool back then...and wouldn't let the memory of Lex impact her now.

The wind rushed past again, rattling the trees and tugging thick sprays of auburn hair from her French braid. Poppy tucked her hair back under her hat. She was a professional, in uniform, with an elite cross-trained poaching and firearms detection K-9 partner by her side. And she had a job to do. No foolish memory of a man who hadn't been ready for commitment was about to shake her focus now. No matter how much she'd once loved him.

Her footsteps strode silently across the mossy ground, moving swiftly from one cabin to the next and letting Stormy take the lead as the wolfhound sniffed for clues. Her phone rang. It was Will, who'd been questioning staff in another part of the park with his K-9 partner about a mile and a half away, where the remnants of drug use had been found. She answered.

"Hey," she said. "Looks like we've still got a cell signal." They'd been warned once they got much farther into the national park cell reception would go dead. "Find anything?"

"Not yet," Will replied. He was a solid trooper, with a knack for handling conflict with humor. But even over the phone, she could hear the tension in his voice. "Have you found anything unusual or out of the ordinary?"

"No, not yet. We've cleared thirteen cabins so far and are approaching the fourteenth now. What kind of unusual should we be on the lookout for?"

Will blew out a breath.

"I don't know exactly," her colleague admitted. "I just have this sense that someone here's not being fully honest with us, about something. I can't tell what. I just know I don't like it."

Stormy growled softly. Poppy glanced down. The dog's posture had straightened, and fur was standing at the back of her neck.

"I've got to go," she said. "Stormy senses something in one of the cabins ahead."

She started toward them slowly. The dog's skill set combined with Poppy's background of working as a wildlife trooper had made them a solid team for investigating illegal hunting and poaching.

"I'm actually done here and heading your way," Will said. Between the shuffle of what sounded like boots on a wooden floor and the jingle of what she guessed were his K-9 partner Scout's dog tags, it sounded like they were already on the move. "I'm going to take one of the park's ATVs."

"Sounds good." She wasn't surprised that he didn't suggest she wait for him. Protocol was that waiting for backup was a judgment call and as Stormy wasn't tracking anyone she didn't expect to find much more than a few bullet cases or maybe some gunpowder. She and Stormy had walked into far worse alone, and Poppy remained endlessly thankful she'd always worked with the kind of folks who didn't treat the male and female troopers any differently in that regard. She'd always been blessed with the people she'd worked with. Even if some, like Lex's former best friend, Johnny Blair, had made some pretty bad life decisions. Alaska was a place where nobody sat around whining and people stepped up to get stuff done. Which is why, even before she'd managed to get the venue and catering deposit back from the canceled wedding that Lex had run out on, she'd already been applying to trooper jobs in Anchorage and packing for a fresh start.

She clenched her jaw. Once again, she was thinking about Lex. *Come on, you're better than that!*

"By the way, there's a park ranger heading your way," Will added. "Says he apparently knows you from back when you worked in Kenai Fjords National Park."

"Okay, thanks." In Alaska, the role of game wardens were played by a specialized type of state trooper, called wildlife troopers. Thankfully, when she'd needed a fresh start, Colonel Lorenza Gallo, one of the first female Alaskan state troopers, had taken her on as part of her incredibly talented and professional K-9 team. Lex might've knocked her down, but thanks to hard work and the kindness of others, she'd definitely landed on her feet.

Stormy growled again and her nose strained toward the next cabin "She's indicating that whatever we're after is in cabin sixteen," Poppy said. "Talk in a bit."

They ended the call and she slid her phone into her jacket pocket. Then she looked down at Stormy. The dog's keen eyes met hers under huge and shaggy brows. There was a floppy, mop-like and almost goofy quality to the huge dog's face that was disarming and friendly. But this was coupled with an intense power, speed and strength that made the dog a formidable foe against hostile people and wild animals alike. "Okay, let's do this. Show me what you've found."

The door swung open at her touch, and the smell of pine filled her senses. Poppy noted that the cabin's main room was simple and empty, with basic wood furniture and two doors ahead. At her signal, Stormy stepped inside and she followed, hearing the floorboards creak beneath their steps. The wolfhound sniffed the air, then signaled toward the second of the closed doors.

Something creaked behind her. The ambush hit swiftly and without warning.

A pair of hands grabbed Poppy by the throat with a tight, pincerlike grip, strangling the air from her lungs and yanking her backward and out of the cabin before she could even reach her weapon. She heard the sound of Stormy barking furiously, a weapon fire and then a door slam, trapping the dog inside the cabin. Desperately, Poppy clawed at the fingers pressing into her windpipe, thrashing against her attacker's grasp and struggling to breathe. Prayers for help surged through her heart. The grip on her throat tightened and darkness swam before her eyes. A male voice swore. Then she felt a second, larger pair of hands grab on to her legs, lifting her up off the ground.

Lex Fielding drove, cutting down the narrow dirt path between the towering trees. Branches slapped the side of his park ranger truck, and rocks spun beneath his wheels. All the while, words cascaded through his mind, clattering and colliding in a mass of disjointed ideas that didn't even begin to come close to what he wanted to say to Poppy. Years ago, he'd had no clue how to explain to the most incredible woman he'd ever known that he didn't think he was ready to get married and have a family. He might not have even had the guts to tell her all his doubts, if she hadn't called him out on it after he'd left a really unfortunate and accidental pocket-dial message on Poppy's voice mail admitting to his mother he wasn't ready to get married. Not that he'd ever told Poppy that's who the conversation had been with.

He'd have thought, as he'd grown and evolved over the past few years, he'd have come up with something better to say to the woman he'd once loved so fiercely than the tired and hollow clichés now filling his mind. *"It's not you, it's me... You were perfect. I was the problem."* Something about being around Poppy had always made him feel like a better man than he had any right being. Even standing beside her made him feel an inch taller. He just hadn't thought he'd been cut out to be anyone's husband. Something he'd then proved a couple of years later by marrying the wrong woman and surviving a couple of unhappy years together before she'd tragically died in a car crash. Yet, amid all that, God had blessed them with a son—an incredible baby boy named Danny, who was now the center of Lex's world.

He heard the chaos ahead before he could even see it through the thick forest. A dog was barking furiously, voices were shouting, and above it all was a loud and relentless banging sound, like something was trying to break down one of the cabins from the inside.

He whispered a prayer and asked God for wisdom. Hadn't been big on prayer outside of church on Sundays back when he'd been planning on marrying Poppy. But ever since Danny had been born, he'd been relying on it more and more to get through the day.

Then the trees parted, just in time to see the two figures directly in front of him dragging something across the road. His heart stopped.

Not something. *Someone.*

They had Poppy.

He swerved hard, almost clipping his truck's right-side mirror as he came to a stop between two trees. His eyes took in the scene in a glance. Both people were in hunting camouflage, their faces obscured by hats and bandannas with only a slit of eyes showing, but at a glance they seemed to be men. A lanky one had Poppy around the shoulders, with one hand clamped over her mouth. His heavier cohort was trying to keep hold of her feet as she kicked and thrashed against them. Her hat had fallen from her head, sending auburn hair flying loose around her face. And above it all, the sound of banging and howling rose. Sounded like they'd locked her K-9 partner in the cabin and the dog was determined to bust out.

He yanked his weapon, leaped from the truck and aimed the firearm between the larger kidnapper's eyes.

"Let her go!" he shouted. "Now!"

The bigger assailant turned, dropping Poppy's feet. But the thinner one yanked her back against him like a human shield with one hand and pulled a gun with the other. Lex rolled as the man fired, his bullet flying into the bushes behind where Lex had been standing. He crouched up behind a tree and hoped he wouldn't have to take a life, even though he would without hesitation to save Poppy.

Long, tense moments passed.

Lex breathed a prayer, then let off a warning shot, sending it high in the canopy of fir branches above their heads. The men froze, like animals did in his truck's headlights in that perilous moment when he didn't know if they were going to flee or charge.

"Park ranger!" Lex shouted. "Let her go. Now!"

Poppy swung her elbows back, hard and fast, catching the man holding her square in the jaw before he could fire again and knocking his camo hat off, revealing a shiny bald head underneath. He grunted, dropped her and then turned and ran for the trees with his beefy accomplice on his heels. Within seconds they'd disappeared into the trees. She crumpled to the ground.

"Poppy!" Her name flew from his lips as he ran for her and dropped to her side like a baseball player sliding home. His arms wrapped around her, pulling her into his chest as he knelt beside her on the ground. Her eyes fluttered closed. *Please, Lord, let her be okay.* He brushed his hand along her cheek, his fingertips tangling in her hair as he felt for her pulse. Red welts rose on her neck from her attacker's grasp. He leaned forward, feeling for the reassurance of her labored breath on his cheek.

"It's okay, Poppy," he rasped. "I'm here. It's me, Lex. I've got you. You're safe."

Her eyes snapped open, deep green and devastatingly beautiful. A pink flush brushed her cheeks. Despite every moment he'd spent trying to convince himself his memories of her were just idealized nonsense, she was even fiercer in person than he'd remembered.

"Lex?" she asked. She reached up and pushed back against his chest. He let her go. "What are you—?"

But before she could finish, a deafening crash filled the air.

TWO

His head snapped toward the cabin in time to see the door smash open, crashing onto the ground. A deep, determined and guttural growl filled the air as a huge mass of gray fur flew toward him. A wolf? A bear? All he knew for sure was that it was barreling into him in a fury, snarling its teeth, knocking him back and pinning him on the ground.

"Stormy!" Poppy's voice rose. "Stand down!"

Instantly the beast leaped off him and sat obediently. Catching his breath, Lex sat up and eyed Poppy's ferocious protector. Stormy was like no dog he'd ever seen before. The Irish wolfhound was huge, with a friendly shaggy face that reminded him of Danny's stuffed toys. Stormy's tail thumped and it looked almost like she was smiling. Then the dog's eyebrows quirked, and she whimpered slightly as if apologizing to him.

For a moment, a well of conflicting emotions seemed to churn in the depths of Poppy's eyes. Tension rose up his spine as he braced himself for a well-deserved tirade from woman he hadn't spoken to since he'd broken her heart days before their wedding. Then she blinked hard, and suddenly the look on her face was so professional it was almost as if he was a stranger.

"I'm sorry about that," Poppy said. "She's really very gentle." Tell that to the cabin door he'd have to fix. Poppy ran her hand over the back of the dog's head. "She'd worked up a pretty big head of steam and probably couldn't stop in time. Trust me, if she'd actually tried to take you down, you'd feel it."

Oh, he already felt it plenty. It was like being hit by a small and furry dirt bike. He stumbled to his feet, hesitated and then reached for Poppy's hand, eyeing Stormy to make sure the K-9 was okay with it. The dog didn't blink.

"Are you okay?" he said. The welts on her neck were already fading, but his chest still ached to remember how vicious the kidnapping attempt had been. "It looked pretty rough."

"I'm fine." Poppy got to her feet without taking his hand. "Trust me, I've handled worse."

He didn't doubt it. She scooped her attacker's camo hat up off the ground, waved it under the dog's nose and told the dog to track it. The wolfhound's ears perked. She woofed enthusiastically and took off running through the forest in the direction the men had gone. He heard the sound of branches crashing in her wake.

"My colleague will be here any second with an ATV," she told him. "I'll take it and go after her. Sometimes, when a K-9's chasing down a suspect, it's better to let them have a head start, than slow them down."

"That's one powerful animal you have there," Lex remarked.

"Stormy is a trooper and my partner," she said. There was something about her tone that almost made him feel reprimanded and he was suddenly reminded of how hard she'd pushed him to apply to become a state trooper himself instead of staying "just" a park ranger. "Irish wolfhounds can run top speed of forty miles an hour, plus she's more adept at running though terrain like this than most people. She'll catch those thugs, unless they've got a vehicle stashed somewhere. If she finds evidence, she'll protect it until I arrive."

He'd seen K-9 troopers let their dogs go in manhunts before, and then follow the sound of a suspect shouting for the dog to let their arm go. Usually they were eager to surrender when the trooper caught up and ordered the dog to release them.

"I didn't know you were a K-9 officer," he admitted, "well, at least not until your partner told me you were the Trooper Walsh who'd flown out from Anchorage with him." After all, she had disappeared pretty thoroughly from his life when he'd called off their engagement.

"Yup." She ran her hands down her legs, and he couldn't tell if she was trying to wipe the dirt off her palms, her slacks or both. "Out of Anchorage. We're a pretty great team."

"I'm really glad," he said quietly. "And congrats. I know how much you wanted to work with the K-9 unit. Not that you weren't incredible at your other job. Honestly, you were the best wildlife trooper I'd ever worked with."

She shot him a sharp glance and Lex hoped he hadn't just implied he was relieved that she hadn't given up a career she was amazing at because of him. That was ridiculous. A woman as driven and determined as Poppy could never have been derailed by a man like him.

"I'm going to go check out the cabin," she said, then turned and stepped over the remains of the broken door. She scooped her phone up off the floor, dialed a number and put it to her ear. "Will," she said. "It's Poppy."

Lex's eyes scanned the cabin as he listened to Poppy fill her fellow trooper in. Her update was simple, straightforward and professional. The cabin was vacant except for an empty carton of bullets, cigarette butts and candy wrappers in the second bedroom. Whoever had been hiding out here hadn't been there long. He spotted her wide-brimmed hat lying on the floor behind the door. He picked it up and then followed her back out. She ended the call, turned to face him, and he felt his breath catch. How could she still have such an impact on him after all these years? Even disheveled and injured, she was even more beautiful, strong and focused than he remembered.

It was unbelievable to think this woman had almost been his wife.

"He'll be here in seconds by the sound of it," she said. "Then he'll search the cabin more thoroughly with his K-9 partner. Scout's a drug-detecting dog."

He held up her hat, she reached for it and their fingertips brushed on the brim. They lingered there, their hands barely touching. He swallowed hard.

"I'm sorry, by the way," he said. "Even if I can't figure out quite how to say it."

A question lingered in her eyes. "Sorry for what?"

Did she really need to hear him say it? They both knew full well what Lex had done. He'd left her out on a limb to plan their wedding entirely by herself, failed to show up for every significant appointment, from catering to venue, and then only admitted he was having cold feet a week before the wedding when she called him out on it.

"For everything," he said.

She paused for a long moment. Her deep green eyes searched his as if looking for something. Then she looked away, tugged the hat from his hands and put it on firmly.

A two-seated ATV pulled into the clearing.

Trooper Will Stryker had dark hair, broad shoulders and the kind of smile that implied he'd also seen his share of pain. His K-9 partner, a black-and-white shaggy border collie, sat on a blanket in a storage basket on the back. Will raised a hand in greeting as Poppy strode over to him.

"Are you okay?" The trooper's eyebrow rose. "Looks like you've been put through the wringer."

"I'm fine," she said. "Mind if I borrow that to go after Stormy?"

"Be my guest." Will hopped off the ATV and signaled for Scout to follow. He nodded to Lex and despite his amiable grin Lex couldn't shake the feeling he was being evaluated. "I hear you two used to work together."

"Actually, we were engaged to be married," Poppy clarified, with a shrug that hit Lex like a punch in the gut. "Didn't work out."

How could she blurt something like that out so casually? Then again, she'd shown practically no emotion when they'd broken up. She hadn't cried, let alone tried to talk him out of calling off the wedding. This woman had been his entire world. Not a day had gone by since he'd regretted breaking her heart.

Hadn't he meant anything to her?

* * *

Moments later, Lex and Poppy were driving through the trees, following the bent branches Stormy had left in her wake. Lex hadn't met her eye since Poppy had told Will that they used to be engaged. Had it bothered him that she'd been so blunt about it? Will was a thorough investigator, as were the rest of her team. If any one of them took a look into Lex it wouldn't be long before someone stumbled onto the fact they'd once been planning to get married. Or maybe she'd blurted it out to show Lex what a good job she'd done getting over him, despite how rattled her heart had been when she'd opened her eyes to find his strong arms around her and his dark, handsome face hovering above hers.

Lex's cell phone buzzed. He pulled it out, glanced at the screen and slid it back into his pocket. Then she heard a familiar woof.

"Stormy!" she called.

The dog was standing guard in a clearing over a set of tire tracks. Poppy leaped off the ATV as Lex pulled to a stop. She signaled to her partner and Stormy trotted over.

"Good dog," she said. Stormy butted her head into Poppy's hand, and she ran her fingers over the back of the dog's shaggy head. "It's okay. We'll get them next time."

Lex climbed off the ATV, got out his phone again and took a picture of the tracks.

"I can send these to you for your team," he offered. "I can tell you right now they're no different from the usual ATV tracks we see from trespassers around here. Despite how vast and remote this place is, we have a major problem with people trespassing and illegal hunting." He frowned, deepening the lines between his eyes, and she was reminded of Will's suspicion that they weren't getting the full story. Was Lex keeping something from them? "Not like this, though."

His phone buzzed again; Lex gave it another swift glanced and didn't answer. Then his phone began to ring and he sent it through to voice mail. Who was so intent on reaching him? And why was he ignoring them?

"You want to tell me what that's about?" she asked, gesturing to his phone.

"Don't worry about it," Lex said. "It's just something I need to sort out."

"But is it related to the poachers?" she pressed. "Because if it is and you're withholding information..."

Her voice trailed off as she watched his jaw set firmly.

"Yes, it might be," he said. "And I will fill you in fully. But later. Please, just give me some time. I need to talk to someone first."

Okay, then. She could hardly force him to tell her what she wanted to know any more than she could force any other witness or source on a case. The trooper inside her still wanted to press him for answers. But the woman who'd once loved this man, and expected to spend the rest of her life with him, knew how much Lex hated being pushed into anything and how stubborn it made him when she tried. Usually the only thing that worked to make him open up was to wait until he'd sorted out whatever was going on inside his brain.

Sometimes not even then, she reminded herself. If it hadn't been for the accidental message he'd left on her answering machine she might've never known he had cold feet about marrying her.

But thinking about that is hardly going to help me with this case now, is it?

There was no way Stormy would fit in the storage cage on the back of the ATV like

Scout had. So they drove back slowly, while Stormy ran alongside.

"I have a source," Lex said after what felt like an extremely long silence. "He tipped me off to the fact that the two poachers had turned on a third poacher and murdered him, and that a bear cub had been captured for illegal sale. I promised I'd try to keep his name out of it and solve this without involving him, if I could. But I warned him it might not be possible."

His phone rang again and once again he declined the call.

"Is that him?" she asked.

Lex didn't answer. He also didn't meet her gaze. An unsettled feeling climbed up her spine that reminded her too much of the past. Right, so he was definitely hiding something.

"Will suspects someone here is not being fully honest with us," she added. "Are you?"

"Hang on," he said. "I might as well brief you both at once."

She could see the cabin up ahead now. Will and Scout were outside waiting for them. Lex stopped the ATV, they got off and she filled Will in about the tire tracks. He hadn't found anything new in the cabins, either.

"Poppy…uh, Trooper Walsh wondered if

there were any significant facts that I might not have filled you in on yet," Lex said, turning to the other man. "As I mentioned to her, I did receive a tip from a local that illegal hunters were poaching bear cubs on one of the glaciers and had killed one of their crew."

"And where did your source get the tip?" Will interjected.

"Claims he overheard someone talking about it at a local hangout," Lex said.

"And is that credible?" Will pressed.

"I believed him." His arms crossed. "Anyway, a colleague and I did an aerial search and spotted a tranquilized mother bear, which we believed to be a black bear. Farther along, we spotted a man's body in the water who turned out to be a known poacher with a long criminal record for illegal hunting and several warrants out in his name. He'd been shot at point-blank range."

This much they'd already known when the team had been called in to investigate from Anchorage, Poppy thought. The fact Lex had a secret source was new, though.

"By the time we returned by boat and retrieved the body, the bear was long gone," Lex continued. "But there was evidence there'd been a second bear cub hiding in a tree nearby. This matched the tip I'd gotten that had said the poachers were after two bear cubs—one of which it seems has now been captured alive to be sold and the other which the poachers are still after."

"Any idea why the poachers turned on each other and killed one of their own?" Poppy asked.

"Money apparently," Lex said. "Greed. Nothing more complicated than one guy just deciding he wanted a bigger piece of the pie."

Poppy thought of the two men who'd attacked her and wondered if that meant one of them would eventually kill the other to keep all the money from the illegal sale for himself.

Will frowned. "No honor among thieves."

Lex ran his hand along the back of his neck.

"There's one more thing," Lex added, "and I'd like you to keep it confidential within your team, please. My source tells me the cub they captured was a blue bear."

Poppy gasped, but her colleague just blinked.

"What's a blue bear?" Will asked.

"Blue bears are also known as glacier bears," Poppy explained. "They're pretty rare and have a silvery gray fur that can look bluish in some lights. They can only be found in Alaska, and people come from all over the world to our national parks in the hopes of seeing one."

She glanced at Lex, wondering if he wanted to add anything; instead, he just nodded as if telling her to keep going. An unfamiliar warmth filled her core. He had always respected her, even when they'd been at their worst.

"They do look a lot like black bears," she added. "Some are only silvery on their underbelly and paws, and there are cases of black bears having blue cubs or vice versa, due to crossbreeding. So, it is completely possible for park wardens to think they'd seen a black mother bear that was tranquilized but that her cubs were blue."

"Right," Lex said. "I hope you can understand why we'd want to keep this news under wraps for now. The news of blue bear cubs would definitely be a huge draw to the national park. But, according to my source, the poachers were as surprised as we are by this and started fighting among themselves when they realized they could get thousands more than they'd expected. They haven't found a buyer yet and want to capture the second cub and sell them together." A muscle ticked in his jaw. "What we don't want to do is put the cubs in further danger or help the poachers jack up the price or attract a wider pool of buyers by publicizing things."

Lex's phone buzzed again. This time he held up a finger and took the call.

"Sorry," he said. "I've got to take this." He took three steps away and held the phone to his ear. "Hey, Mom. What's up?… Uh-huh… Yup… Okay, I'm on my way. Tell him Daddy will be there soon."

Daddy? The single word seemed to knock the air from Poppy's lungs. *The man who wouldn't start a family with her was now a father?*

Lex turned back; his face had paled, and although he glanced at both her and Will, something made her feel like his words were directed to her alone.

"I've got to go," Lex said. "I have a son. His name is Danny. He's two and my mom thinks she saw someone watching him over the back fence."

THREE

Poppy felt her lips part but no words come out. She'd longed to have a child back when they were engaged and had spent hours agonizing over the fact she desperately wanted to start a family and Lex didn't. Finally, she'd made peace with marrying him, anyway, praying that one day God would change his heart and he'd be ready.

Instead, he'd started a family with someone else.

"Do you think there's a connection between someone spying on your son and the poaching case?" Will asked. Gratitude flooded over her that her colleague was focusing on what mattered even while she was left reeling.

"I expect so," Lex said, and started walking back toward his truck. His voice was grave. "It's too much of a coincidence to be otherwise."

Poppy forced herself to pray for focus. This was about so much more than her own broken heart or the shattered dreams of her past. Stormy's head butted against her leg. She reached down and ran her hand through her partner's soft fur.

"One of us should go with you," Will said.

"It should be me," Poppy announced, heading for the truck. "Stormy is trained in tracking people. If whoever was watching Lex's son left anything behind, Stormy and I can track them."

Lex hesitated a moment and then he nodded. "Yeah, you're right."

He opened the back door of his truck for Stormy to climb inside. It was only then that Poppy noticed the car seat strapped in the back. Stormy curled up into a ball on the seat beside it. Poppy told Will she'd check in with him later and got in the passenger side, and then they were off.

For a long moment, Lex didn't say anything. Neither did she. Instead, she turned her eyes toward the window and watched the trees as they drove past. What could she even say? Lex had known he'd been the only man in the entire world she'd wanted to have a family with when he'd rejected her and called off their wedding. And their past didn't even rank up there in the top three things she had to worry about right now. They drove through the main gates of Glacier Bay National Park and started toward the tiny town of Gustavus.

"I've spent so much time trying to figure out how I'd ever tell you about this," Lex admitted gruffly. "Even now, I have no idea where to start…"

The sound of his voice turned her attention back to his face. He was staring straight ahead. His eyes were locked on the road in front of him and his hands gripped the wheel exactly at ten and two. She hadn't even thought to check for a wedding ring, but now noticed he wasn't wearing one.

"I met Debra through mutual friends about a year and a half after you and I stopped seeing each other." He spoke quickly, like he was giving a necessary briefing of unpleasant information he didn't want to convey. Not like a man with feelings who had a heart beating in his chest that had ever loved someone. "We fought a lot and she had a lot of personal problems. I thought getting married would fix things. It didn't. Then I thought having a baby would make things better."

His voice trailed off and he sighed. Poppy waited.

"She started traveling to Juneau after Danny was born to see her mother," he continued. "When Danny was six months old, she admitted she thought marrying me had been a mistake. She hated living here and we were separated when she died in a car crash. She'd been driving on a rural road, late at night, in a storm. It looks like either a bear or some other large animal charged at her car and she swerved off the road trying to avoid it. Not her fault. Debra was an anxious driver and it was just one of those tragic accidents that could happen to anyone on these roads. Mom moved out here to help me raise Danny."

He fell quiet again for a long moment.

"I'm sorry," she said eventually, not really knowing what else to say.

"I don't want to sound like I'm putting all the blame on her," he said. "For the failed marriage, I mean. I've spent a lot of time in prayer asking God to forgive me for my shortcomings and examining the mistakes I made so I could become a better man."

There was something about the way he said

it that made her think that maybe he hadn't forgiven himself yet.

"She really loved Danny," Lex went on, "and Gustavus isn't an easy place to live. It takes a certain type of person to choose to be happy here. Debra loved it in the summer when the town was full of thousands of tourists. It's a lot harder in the winter, though, when it's dark and cold all day, and only a few hundred people."

He pulled the truck to a stop at the side of the road, then turned and looked at her.

"I don't expect you to understand," Lex said. "But after I got cold feet with you, I was so afraid of making the same mistake twice that I jumped in too fast with Debra and made other mistakes."

For a moment, his eyes lingered on hers. The space between them seemed to shrink.

Was he saying that not marrying her had been a mistake?

He opened the truck door and got out, waving her to follow. She looked up. They were parked outside a large three-story house that looked like a lodge. Cheerful wind chimes hung from the long and covered front porch. A tiny calico kitten, not much bigger than a teacup, was curled up in the large front window and a wooden sign out front welcomed her to the Hope's Nest Bed and Breakfast. Poppy got out, opened the back door and signaled for Stormy to join her. Then she hung back by the truck and watched as Lex hurried up the steps of the sprawling wooden front porch.

The door opened and Lex's mother stepped out, her long gray hair tied back in a bun and a warm smile on her face. A little boy with short and tousled brown hair that seemed to stick up in all possible directions wriggled in her hold, squealing and reaching out for his father as Lex grew closer. Moments later, Lex gathered Danny into his arms, and the toddler snuggled against him as he whispered something into the little boy's ear.

Something tugged painfully in her heart. She'd always suspected that Lex would be a wonderful father. It was another thing to see it with her own eyes.

Lex turned and started down the front steps toward Poppy, with his son in his clutches and his mother in tow.

"Poppy, this is my son, Danny," he said. His smile beamed. "And you remember my mother, Gillian."

"I do." She'd always gotten along so well

with Lex's mom that Gillian had even stepped
in to help with things like dealing with the
wedding venue and arranging the seating plan
when Lex hadn't. If Poppy was honest, she'd
been surprised Gillian hadn't managed to talk
her son into not calling off the wedding. She
hesitated for a moment, not quite knowing
if she should shake the older woman's hand
or hug her. But Gillian opened her arms and
stepped forward.

"Welcome, Poppy!" Lex's mother said.
Happiness crinkled her eyes as they em-
braced. "It's so wonderful that you're the one
who was sent here to help Lex with this case."

Something about her tone left Poppy wondering if Gillian thought God had sent her.

"Doggy!" Danny squealed, and waved both
hands toward Stormy.

Poppy felt a smile cross her lips.

"Her name is Stormy," she said. "She's a
very special dog."

"Big doggy!" The toddler's eyes grew
wide. "Big and f'uffy."

"Yes," she murmured. "Stormy is very big
and fluffy."

Lex chuckled softly and led them around
the side of the house. The yard was surrounded by a four-foot-tall fence. Poppy no-

ticed the gate had a solid clasp but wasn't locked.

"Where are you and Stormy staying?" Gillian asked her.

"My colleague, Will Stryker, and I are staying at a motel just outside of town," she said. "It was the only place open that allowed dogs."

"Ugh, that place," Gillian said. Her nose wrinkled, and Poppy wasn't surprised. The motel was pretty run-down and didn't smell all that great, either. They'd be having their team meeting by video chat on a rickety metal folding table later that night. She hadn't even unpacked yet. "Well, you and Will, and your dogs, are very welcome to stay here."

"Thank you," Poppy said. "I really appreciate it."

Not that she was planning on taking Lex's mother up on the offer.

Suddenly finding herself face-to-face with Lex after all these years was already wreaking more than enough havoc on her heart and mind. Staying with him, his mother and adorable little son was more than she could handle.

"He was right over here," Gillian indicated. They crossed the backyard, passing a child's playhouse, swing set and sandbox, and walked over to the fence. "Danny was playing in the sand and I was watching him from the back porch when I saw a large a man in a camo hunting jacket standing right over here. He had a bandanna over this face. I called out to him and he ran."

Sounded just like one of her two kidnappers. Poppy glanced at Lex and watched as he shuddered. She climbed the back fence and directed Stormy to follow. The dog leaped over in a bound and started sniffing the area. But after a few minutes of searching, both she and the dog came up empty. They rejoined her ex and his family on the other side.

"And you're sure he was watching Danny?" Lex asked.

"Sure seemed that way," Gillian said. "I wondered at first if he was an early tourist walking around. But he had his hat pulled pretty low over his head and that bandanna pulled up over his face. If I hadn't known any better, I would've thought it was your friend Johnny. But even though Johnny hasn't been around in a while I'd have hoped he'd have known to just walk up and said hi."

Poppy froze.

Did she mean Johnny Blair? He was back

in Lex's life? Lex's friend from childhood had worked with them both at the national park, before he'd been fired for stealing months before the wedding. That on top of a rap sheet full of trouble including selling cigarettes to tourists younger than twenty-one, poaching small animals and hustling tourists at darts and pool. Last she'd heard, the two men were estranged and had fallen out of touch.

Even then, Lex had insisted on dropping by in person to invite Johnny to their wedding when he didn't respond to RSVP to his invitation despite the bad blood with those they'd worked with.

It had been one of the last things she and Lex had fought about. Especially after Lex refused to either confirm or deny that Johnny had been the person he'd been admitting his doubts to on that pocket-dial message that had led to their breakup. Lex said it didn't actually matter who he'd been talking to when he confessed that he sometimes wanted to call off the wedding. But Poppy had suspected that whoever it was had talked Lex into ending it.

She waited until Gillian turned and walked back to the house.

"Johnny's here in Gustavus?" she asked.

"What is he doing here? Is that who you've been hiding calls from? Tell me he's not your source."

Lex didn't answer, but one glance in his eyes told her everything she needed to know.

Johnny Blair, the deadbeat former friend with a criminal record who she suspected might've talked Lex into ending their engagement, was also the one who'd told Lex about the blue bear poachers.

Something hardened in Lex's heart as he watched Poppy's lip curl. For all her wonderful qualities, she'd never understood why he'd never given up on Johnny, despite the mistakes he'd made. She didn't get how people who were in a rough place in life needed someone who believed in them and didn't shut them out. Things had always come so easy for her—reaching goals, achieving in school, standing out and getting hired. She'd never known what it was like to struggle with things, let alone need a second chance.

Which might be why Lex had never thought to ask her for one.

His mother had gone into the house, no doubt to put the kettle on and rustle up some cookies. Which gave the two of them time to talk privately.

"Yes," he said. "Johnny moved out here last year when he'd fallen on hard times. We hadn't talked in a while and I was hoping getting away from the temptations in Anchorage would help him restart his life. I tried to get him a job at the park, but it didn't work out." Lex blew out a breath. "He met a woman, who was also new to town, and they hit it off. He got a job doing maintenance for her brother's new air-tourism charter business and stayed to be with her. Johnny said he didn't want trouble, so I promised to keep his name out of it, if I could."

Which Lex might not be able to do anymore now that Poppy had been attacked.

"He's got a criminal record," Poppy reminded him. She didn't even try to hide the disdain in her voice.

"He's a man who's made some mistakes and is trying to get his life back together." Like Lex himself had with the grace of God and the help of people like his mother. Although, thankfully, he had never gotten involved in illegal activity or anything remotely like that. "We're not particularly close now, truth be told. Hadn't seen him in months when he dropped by one night and told me he'd overheard some out-of-towners talking about poaching baby bear cubs down at the local watering hole."

"So a bar?" Poppy asked. "So, he's back to drinking and hustling tourists again?"

She could've at least tried to camouflage the disgust in her voice. Truth was, Johnny had promised Lex up and down for months that he'd stopped drinking or going to places like that. Which is why Lex had been so shocked and disappointed when Johnny had shamefacedly told him that was where he'd gotten his intel. He almost hadn't wanted to believe it.

"It's not an official bar," Lex said. "One of the local guys has a big triple garage out back of his farm, with some picnic tables and a fire pit, that he sort of runs an unlicensed hangout at."

Poppy rolled her eyes. "Perfect."

He fought the urge to try to explain, yet again, why trying to lend a helping hand to old pals like Johnny mattered so much to him. Truth was, back when he and Poppy had been dating in Anchorage, their evenings together had all too often been interrupted by some former friend or another that Lex hadn't spoken to in eons who needed to be bailed out of jail for fighting or given a ride home after getting too drunk to drive. He hadn't minded. Thanks to his mom's strong faith and strict rules while he was growing up, Lex knew he was the token "good guy" from that old bunch people still knew they could call on.

But she didn't get it.

How *could* she? Poppy hadn't gone through hardship like he had. She didn't know what it was like to grow up poor, have her father walk out and be reliant on the kindness of others. Moreover, she had no clue what it was like to barely make it through school and struggle to make ends meet, or to have to put her life back together after it fell apart. So yes, the truth also was that Johnny had been texting and calling repeatedly for the past half hour, and Lex hadn't called him back because he figured it was less important than what was going on with Poppy.

Danny squirmed in his arms to be put down. Lex complied, without even realizing the toddler would make a beeline for Stormy as fast as his little legs would take him.

"Big doggy!" he squealed.

"Danny!" Lex started after him.

But before he could catch the little boy,

Poppy waved her hand in a quick and furtive motion. Immediately the dog dropped to the ground, lying on its stomach in front of the little boy. Danny barreled into Stormy, head-butting the dog in greeting and then throwing his arms around her. Stormy licked the boy's cheek gently. Danny giggled and flopped onto the grass beside Stormy, his arms still locked around the dog's neck. "Doggy like me, Daddy! Doggy very silly!"

Lex exhaled.

"Stormy's great with children," Poppy said softly under her breath.

He watched as his tiny son and the huge dog rolled together on the grass.

"Thanks for that signal thing you did that got her to drop and for letting him play with her," he said. "Sorry, I didn't think to ask before setting him down."

"No problem." Something seemed to soften in her gaze as she watched Danny and the wolfhound play together. "You need to let me talk to Johnny," she added. "Regardless of our history, I'm a state trooper, I'm investigating this case and he has information about poaching and a murder."

"I know," Lex acknowledged. "You're right." He'd just been hoping he wouldn't have to ask that of Johnny. His friend didn't trust the authorities and would likely see it as a betrayal. "I agree it has to be done."

"Or Will Stryker could do it," she offered.

"No, it should be you," he said, turning to face her. "I know you think Johnny never liked you, but he always did respect you."

His phone was buzzing and even without glancing at the screen he knew from the ringtone it was Johnny calling again. There was no time like the present.

He cleared his throat, then answered.

"Hey, Johnny," he said. "Sorry for not calling back sooner. But you'll never guess who I'm standing next to."

"Lex?" The voice was female, breathless, panicked and full of tears.

"Ripley?" Lex asked. Why did Johnny's girlfriend have his phone? "Are you okay? What's going on? Where's Johnny?"

She gasped a sob.

"A man broke into Johnny's house," she said. "He locked me in a cupboard and got Johnny tied up in the kitchen. He's threatening to kill him if he doesn't tell them who he told about the blue bears."

FOUR

Poppy watched as Lex's face paled. He turned and ran back across the yard.

"Stay hidden!" he called into the phone. "Don't make a sound. I'm on my way."

She had no clue who Ripley was or where Lex was running to. But the look on his face told her everything she needed to know. Someone's life was in danger and Lex was determined to save her. Poppy signaled to Stormy and in an instant her K-9 partner was by her side.

"Whatever happens don't hang up," Lex was telling Ripley. In a seamless motion he scooped Danny up with one arm and cradled him to his chest as he sprinted toward the house. Without a word, Gillian stepped back out onto the back porch and Lex slid Danny into her arms.

"Everything okay?" Lex's mother asked.

Lex shook his head. "Johnny and his girl-friend are in trouble."

"Go," Gillian said. "I'll take Danny and go to a friend's house for now until I hear from you. Stay safe."

Countless questions cascaded through Poppy's mind as she watched Lex take in whatever Ripley was telling him about the situation. Then Lex's dark eyes shot her a glance that answered the only one that mattered right now.

"Please come with me," he said. "I need your help."

She nodded and they ran around the house and back through the gate, with Stormy by her side and Lex one pace ahead of her. They reached his truck, and he threw open the passenger side door for her and the back door for Stormy before hurrying around to the driver's side.

"You need to stay quiet," Lex told Ripley. "I'm going to put my end of the call on mute so none of what's going on here comes through the phone. But I'm still here, I'm still listening and I'm on my way. I promise."

Poppy shut Stormy's door, then hopped in, closed her own and secured her seat belt. Lex slid the phone into his truck's hands-free holster and started the engine.

"So, again, Ripley is Johnny's girlfriend?" she asked.

"She is," Lex confirmed. He gripped the steering wheel so tightly his knuckles were white. His eyes locked on the road ahead. "She filled me in as much as she could, which isn't much. Here's what I know. Ripley said a man broke into Johnny's house, tied him up and threatened to kill him if he didn't tell them who all he told about the blue bears."

In other words: Lex.

She glanced at Stormy in the rearview mirror. The dog was sitting alert in the back seat, with her ears perked and her keen eyes on Poppy, ready to get to work and leap into action. She wondered what it was like to have as much unwavering trust in anyone as Stormy did in her.

"Do we have a description?" she asked.

"No, but she says he was disguised in camo."

Same as the two who'd tried to kidnap her in the national park.

"Ripley says he forced her into the living room cupboard and locked her in," Lex added.

"Thankfully she found Johnny's phone in his jacket pocket."

"I'm calling Will," she said, "and getting him to meet us there."

Her colleague's phone went straight through to voice mail. Not surprising, based on how unreliable cell signals could be in the area. She relayed the details and how to find Johnny's place in a phone message as Lex rattled them off to her, and then after she hung up, sent him the same details in a text. Poppy wished she'd been able to reach him and couldn't shake the feeling that Will would've had his own out-of-the-box perspective on things, which would've helped equip her for whatever it was they were about to walk into. She'd always liked to get input from others. Even when she thought it was wrong. Which is why Lex's inability to talk through things back in the day had been so hard.

Come on, think. She closed her eyes. *What would the others on my team notice that I've missed?*

They'd have probably honed in on Johnny's criminal record. Then maybe they'd have pointed out that, just like one of Poppy's attackers, Johnny had always been a beefy guy—something Gillian had just confirmed when she'd said the person on the other side of the fence had looked like him. Because of that coincidence they might've told her to be aware she could now be walking into a setup.

Then again, she'd always thought Johnny genuinely cared about his estranged friend. Would Johnny really lie to Lex and risk putting his pal's life in danger?

She opened her eyes to see an empty rural road and a sea of trees.

"Does Ripley have a history with police?" she asked.

"I don't know," Lex said. "We've never really spoken. I just know Johnny is very protective of her and she moved here from Juneau with her brother, Nolan, to get away from an ex-boyfriend who treated her badly."

"Why did she call you?" she asked.

"Guessing her brother is off giving some people an aerial tour of the glaciers," Lex said. "His airfield's in a pretty remote area."

"But why *you*?" she pressed.

"There's no local law enforcement in Gustavus," Lex said. "Town actually took a vote and decided against it. We do have 911, but it connects you to the fire department, medical emergency or search and rescue. They're all

run by volunteers. Anything park-related falls
on us park rangers and for anything major we
call in the troopers who fly in from Juneau or
Anchorage. Like you." He glanced her way
and the faintest hint of a sad grin hovered on
the edge of his mouth, then it faded again.
"No local government, building permits, by-
laws or property taxes, either. Gustavus is an
interesting place. But it's not for everyone."

His brow furrowed. They drove past scat-
tered buildings as eight minutes ticked by one
slow and drawn-out eternity at a time. Silence
had fallen from Ripley's end of the phone.
Lex took it off mute.

"Ripley?" he called softly. "I'm on my way
and almost there. Are you okay?"

No answer. Just some faint and indistinct
scuffling sounds came down the phone line.
Poppy's heart clenched.

"Ripley." Lex's tone grew urgent. "Can you
hear me?"

"Yeah, I'm here." Ripley's voice was soft
and terrified. "I'm locked in the cupboard so
I can't get out and I can't hear Johnny or anyone anymore."

Lex exhaled. "Just hang tight. I'll be there
soon."

Poppy barely saw the unmarked break in

the trees before he turned into it and onto an unpaved track so long and narrow she couldn't tell if it was a road or a driveway. Stormy woofed softly, with just the hint of a growl like the threat of an approaching storm.

"What's that?" Ripley's voice rose.

"My friend's dog," Lex said, his voice both soothing and firm like he was trying to reassure a frightened animal. "Don't worry. She's a really great dog and completely gentle and safe. Now just stay calm and hold on. It's going to be okay."

Suddenly the phone went dead and any remaining hint of color drained from Lex's face.

Prayers poured from his lips, asking God to help them reach Ripley and Johnny in time, and she found herself fighting the urge to reach across the front seat and squeeze his hand.

Suddenly it hit her just how dire the situation was. Out here in the wilderness there was no backup, no law enforcement and no team of police about to sweep in and save the day.

All Lex had was her.

Then she saw the ranch house. It was old and run-down with a sloping roof that was missing a few shingles and yet its structure still implying how majestic a home it had once been. The carcasses of half-built and unbuilt trucks, boats, motorcycles and trailers littered the lawn. Clothes fluttered on a long laundry line. Lex pulled to a stop and jumped out. Poppy checked her phone, saw no message from Will and then ran around to the back door and opened it for Stormy. Her partner leaped out and Poppy was amazed anew at how smoothly and silently she could move for an animal her size.

She clipped Stormy's leash on her harness and ran her hand over the soft fur at the back of the dog's neck and said, "Let's go."

Immediately the dog stretched and rose to her full height like a mythical wolf preparing for battle. Lex started toward the house, then crouched low behind a car chassis. Poppy instinctively grabbed a red T-shirt off the clothesline as they moved to join him, in case they needed to get Stormy to track Johnny's scent. Even without giving the dog the command to search, she felt the leash tighten slightly with a pressure as subtle as one dancer guiding the other on the dance floor. She looked down at Stormy. The dog's snout was pointing farther down the dirt road away from the house. What did she sense?

"I don't see anything through the windows and the curtains are drawn," Lex said, "and I'm not hearing so much as a floorboard creak, so we've got no idea what's going on in there. But Ripley said she's hiding in the living room closet and that they're holding Johnny in the kitchen. I suggest that I go in through the front door and you head in around the back."

She resisted the urge to point out that she was the cop, not him. Despite the fact, she'd encouraged him several times to apply to become a wilderness trooper, considering how good he was with animals, calm and steady under pressure, and skilled at both knowing his way around a weapon and dealing with life-threatening adversaries from bears to drunkenly violent tourists. Stormy tugged the leash slightly harder as if to imply she had an opinion, too.

Poppy waved the shirt under the K-9's nose and whispered, "Search."

Immediately Stormy straightened, turned toward the path and woofed.

"What's down there?" Poppy asked.

"An old barn Johnny sometimes uses as a garage slash workshop," Lex said.

"Well, Stormy thinks we need to head there."

"Okay, we can definitely check that out after the farmhouse."

"No," Poppy said. "I just gave Stormy a T-shirt off the clothesline to sniff and she thinks we should go there instead of the farmhouse."

"No offense intended," Lex said as his eyes met hers. "But she could be smelling anything off that shirt, and I think that's the wrong call."

He watched as Poppy's eyes widened. He hadn't actually meant to offend her, but figuring out the right words to say had never been his strong suit. Poppy had never shied away from jumping in and taking charge of things. And it's not like they had time to argue.

"Stormy's not some pet." Her chin rose. "She's a highly trained state trooper."

"I know that—" he started.

"And if she thinks we need to head down the path, that's good enough for me."

Lex glanced from Poppy, to the house and then to his phone. It had been barely six minutes since Ripley's call had gone dead and he still had no idea what was going on inside there beyond what she'd told him. He gritted his teeth.

"I get that," he said, "but it's also not like

she has X-ray vision and can tell us what's going on in that house."

Something flashed in the green depths of Poppy's eyes, determined and strong, like she was gearing up for a fight. In the months after losing her, he'd started coming to terms with just how much his fear of arguing with her had wrecked and scuttled any hope of a real relationship with her.

Now, it could be an actual matter of life or death.

"Let's just split up," he said. "You and Stormy head down the path and I'll go to the farmhouse."

"But we'll be stronger and more effective together," she protested.

Maybe, but not if they couldn't agree on a plan and just stood around arguing.

"Poppy," Lex said. "You know as well as I do that we were never very good at acting like a team."

He watched as some kind of mental calculation seemed to flicker in her eyes. And realized this might actually be the first time he'd openly disagreed with her on anything instead of either just nodding along or cutting bait just to avoid a fight. Stormy growled, softly, like the tremor of a distant earthquake shaking the ground. Then to his surprise, Poppy nodded.

"Fair enough," she said. "You take the house and we'll follow the scent. Stay safe, Lex."

"You, too."

She turned and ran down the path with her body low and Stormy just one step ahead of her. In an instant he'd lost sight of them in the trees. He turned toward the house. Doubt trickled down the back of his neck. What if he was wrong and Poppy was right? Either way one of them was heading into danger without the other as backup. He prayed it wasn't her.

He slipped around the side of the house, straining his ears for any hint of activity inside. There was nothing. The back door to the kitchen lay open and his heart sank as he glanced inside. The room was empty, with only a few broken dishes and a single kitchen chair fallen over on its side in the middle of the room to show there'd even been a struggle. He kept praying and pushed the door open, feeling a slight resistance on the handle as if something was holding it back.

The resistance snapped, a twang sounded and instinctively Lex leaped back as something flew past within an inch of his nose and embedded itself in the wall beside him. It was a tranquilizer dart, the kind that poachers used to take out bears and large enough to knock a big person down for a long time and put a smaller one in the hospital. His heart thudded. Someone had boobytrapped Johnny's house.

Had Johnny been worried that someone was after for him? Or had his kidnappers laid a trap for whoever came to rescue him?

"Help!" The voice was female, muffled and seemed to be coming from the living room. "Help me! Please! I'm in here!"

Ripley.

He steeled a breath and cautiously moved through the kitchen to the living room, looking out for other traps as he went.

The living room was empty and dark; the drawn curtains fairly effectively blocked out the light.

He reached the cupboard door. Someone had fastened a crude padlock to its double doors locking it shut.

"Move back," Lex called. "I'm going to break it down!"

He leveled a swift kick at the doors, catching them right above the lock. The cheap wood splintered, the door handles snapped off and the cupboard fell open.

"Lex!" Ripley emerged from behind a shield of coats and outdoor gear. Her long dark hair was tied back in two disheveled braids and makeup ran from her tearstained eyes, making her slender form look years younger than the midtwenties he knew her to be. "I'm so glad you're here!"

A gag lay loose around her neck and as she stepped out into the living room he could see faint welts on her wrists.

"He tied you up and gagged you?" Lex asked.

Ripley nodded. "With bandannas. But I was able to rip them on the edge of Johnny's toolbox, get my hands free and then take off the gag."

And then find Johnny's phone, Lex thought.

"How long have you been in here?" he asked.

"I don't know," she said. "Where's Johnny?"

"I was about to ask you that," Lex said.

Her eyes widened. "I thought someone dragged him into the kitchen."

"Maybe so, but he's not there now."

The front porch creaked. In an instant, Lex threw himself in front of his buddy's girlfriend, pushing Ripley behind him. The door flew open, and two more darts twanged, imbedding themselves in the wooden door as it suddenly shut again. Then the door swung back open again and Lex looked to see the tall, broad-shouldered form of a man standing there silhouetted against the sun.

"Lex," Will said as he stepped into the room, then gave a signal and his border collie partner sprung to his side. "Sorry, I got here as fast as I could. What do you need? Has the scene been secured? Where's Poppy?"

There was something about the man's sharp and focused professionalism that immediately put Lex at ease, while also reminding him of the type of man Lex had always suspected Poppy wanted him to be. Especially after seeing how smoothly Will had dodged the trap.

"The kitchen and living room are secured, but I haven't checked the rest of the house," Lex added. "The back door was also rigged with a tranquilizer dart and I don't know if there are more."

"Do we know why?" Will asked, glancing at the projectile embedded in the door frame.

Lex looked at Ripley. "Do you?"

She shook her head but didn't meet his

eye. Okay, so that was something he'd have to question more later.

"When I last saw Poppy and Stormy they were headed to the back of the property," Lex added. "I have to find her."

He needed to. In a way he didn't even understand. It was like his heart was aching to know that Poppy was okay and hadn't walked directly into a trap.

"Ripley, this is Trooper Will Stryker and his K-9 partner, Scout," Lex added, stepping to the side to allow introductions. "Ripley is the one who called me about Johnny Blair's abduction. Johnny was my source about the poaching of the blue bear cubs."

"Please to meet you," Will said. "I'm glad to see you're all right." Lex watched as the trooper stretched out his hand as if to shake Ripley's, but when she hesitated, he pulled it back and simply nodded to her instead. The whole motion had been seamless. "You find Poppy. Scout and I will stay with Ripley and secure the house."

"Sounds good," Lex said. A fleeting thought crossed his mind that Will still might not trust him and was trying to keep him away from Ripley while he took her statement. But in that moment he didn't care. All that mattered was that Poppy was all right. He ran outside and down the path in the direction she and Stormy had disappeared.

The sound of a shotgun exploded ahead of him with what he guessed was buckshot pelting its target. His heartbeat quickened as prayers pounded through his chest with every step. Then he saw Poppy running toward him. Her green eyes were wide in her pale face.

He knew in an instant something was wrong.

"Lex!" His name escaped her lips in a gasp.

His arms opened instinctively, and she crashed into them. She clutched him to her in a tight hug as his own embrace closed around her. There'd always been a mightiness to her hugs. It was like she could see the disjointed pieces of him and was helping him set the glue that held them all together.

Her hugs had made him feel stronger.

"I heard gunshots," he said.

"The garage was rigged with booby traps," she explained. "Both tranquilizer darts and a shotgun."

"House was boobytrapped too," he said. "I don't know if Johnny was expecting trouble or if his kidnapper was trying to kill whoever came to rescue him. You okay?"

"Yeah," she said. "Thankfully Stormy sniffed them out."

He thanked God for Stormy and was about to ask where she was when he caught sight of her over Poppy's shoulder sitting at attention in front of the garage.

Poppy pulled back enough to look in his face.

"Oh, Lex, I'm so sorry—" she began.

"Hey, hey, it's okay."

His hand slid to her cheek and cupped it in his fingers. But her head shook away from his touch.

"It's Johnny." Pained filled Poppy's voice. "Oh, Lex, I'm so sorry. But Johnny's dead."

FIVE

Thunder rumbled in the distance, warning of impending rain. Lex stood alone in the doorway of the dilapidated garage and looked at his buddy's body from a distance, feeling sorrow heavy like a lead weight in his chest. Johnny's large form sat slumped in a sagging lawn chair, with his hands tied behind his back and his head resting over his chest almost as if he was asleep. A single gunshot wound made it clear the death had been instantaneous and he'd probably been killed even before Ripley had managed to get her hands free enough to call him.

Lord, have mercy on him, his family and everyone who loves him. Lex prayed. Johnny had been heading down the wrong path for so very long. Lex wished that he and his old buddy had been closer in the past couple of years, and that he'd been able to do more to help him before it was too late. He hoped Johnny had found the redemption he'd sought in his final moments.

Poppy and Stormy had stayed outside and left him to go in alone to confirm it was Johnny and give him a moment. But as he walked back outside and into the trees, in such a daze he could barely see the world around him, he felt Poppy step beside him. Instinctively his hand reached for hers; she took it and their fingers linked. He stood there, looking up at the clouds building above him and holding Poppy's hand. For a moment he didn't know what words to say or even how to turn and look into her eyes, but somehow just standing there feeling her touch was enough.

"There's nothing you could've done," Poppy whispered.

His hand slipped from hers. Stormy buffeted her head softly against his other side as if she sensed his sadness, too, and wanted to make sure he was okay. He ran his hand over the dog's head.

"I know," he said, not even sure if she was talking about the fact the call had come too late for him to save Johnny or the complicated, two-decades-long friendship he and Johnny had. "We haven't been close in years and every time he disappeared I steeled my-self for the fact I might never see him again." He turned toward her. "At least this way I can help ensure his killer is brought to justice."

"And you will," Poppy said as her green eyes met his, unflinching and uncompromis-ing. "I promise you that."

He believed her and he'd forgotten how good it felt to have someone like her by his side.

"Will has secured the house and is taking Ripley's statement," she added. "We've called in troopers from Juneau to airlift Johnny's body to the morgue there for an autopsy. But we didn't know who we should call locally."

"My mother," he said, and watched as she blinked. "As a retired emergency room nurse she's the most qualified medical professional in town. Also, the volunteer firefighters can help secure the area to make sure no one gets in or out."

He paced a few steps back in the direction of the house and ran one hand through his hair, feeling a mental switch flip inside him. Later, he'd mourn the loss of his friend. But right now, he had to turn his feelings off—including the confusing ones being around

Poppy stirred up in him—and he started mentally listing the things that needed to happen.

"I'm going to call my mom and explain the situation," he said. "She'll get a trusted friend to watch Danny while she drives out here. You said Will is taking Ripley's statement. I also need to call her brother, Nolan, if no one's informed him yet and let him know what's happened. He runs a small charter airline business and she says he's off flying someone to Juneau today but should be back soon. She lives with him, and while I don't really know him, he's always seemed very protective. You mentioned state troopers from Juneau are coming to take Johnny to the medical examiner's office. What am I forgetting?"

"Nothing," Poppy reassured him. "I also need to call my boss, Colonel Lorenza Gallo, in Anchorage and brief her as the Alaskan K-9 unit officially has jurisdiction of the case. But I'm sure she'll have no problem coordinating with Juneau."

The gray-haired woman with a stylish pixie cut and what he seemed to remember was an affinity for interesting jewelry came to mind. He'd met Lorenza once when, unbeknownst to Poppy, he'd attended an Alaska trooper recruitment event in Anchorage while they were still engaged. Poppy had been pressing him to consider applying to become a wildlife trooper, despite the fact he didn't really have the educational background for it and had never been a big fan of school. Lorenza had been the one who told him he seemed to be really happy as a park ranger, and that he should be in a job that called to him. Poppy's boss had kind of reminded him of his mother.

"Will and I are scheduled to have a video call with my team tonight," Poppy added. "You should give Will an official statement, as well. We need you to go on the record about what Johnny told you, and it's better that Will be the one who takes the statement."

Right, because of their history.

He glanced over at where Stormy now sat, patiently and contentedly waiting for direction.

"You think I should apologize to Stormy for not following her lead?" he asked.

He'd meant it as a feeble joke to lighten the tension, but Poppy's lips didn't even twitch.

"No, there were only two of us, and it made sense to split up." She frowned. "Lex, are you sure you know that none of this is your fault?"

"You're repeating yourself." He shrugged. "You said that before."

"And I want to be doubly certain that you hear me," she said. "The killer was long gone before we got here. You could've run off to the garage the moment we pulled up and it wouldn't have made a difference. Plus, I know better than anyone how hard you've worked to be there for your friends. I was there all those times you ran out of the movies or skipped out on dinner because Johnny or somebody else needed you. I was there when you lent your friends money or vouched for them to get jobs. I also know that you're really good at pushing your emotions down and just getting on with things. I want to make sure you're okay."

She was one to talk. Poppy hadn't even seemed upset when he'd broken off their engagement. Then again, she could probably say the same about him, despite the fact his heart had been breaking. A breeze brushed through the space between them.

"Thank you," he said gruffly. "But I'm fine."

He turned and walked back to the house, pulling out his phone as he went and gritting his teeth.

Maybe she was right. Maybe he wasn't okay and hadn't been for a long while. But if he fell apart now there was no way of knowing what emotions would suddenly come spilling out.

And if that happened, he couldn't afford it to be in front of Poppy.

The sun had dipped lower behind the ominous clouds when Poppy finally finished securing the scene at Johnny's house and was able to take Stormy for a quick jog around the motel where she and Will were staying. A dog Stormy's size would definitely need a second, much longer run than the small gap of time Poppy had before her video team meeting would allow. But she needed the time alone to think and pray.

If she was honest, she'd never really liked Johnny. She'd never particularly cared for any of Lex's friends from childhood. They were reckless, immature, underemployed and content calling on Lex to bail them out instead of taking responsibility for their own mistakes.

But, Lord, I need Your help to make sure my own biases don't cloud my judgment here. I ask You to bless Johnny's family and everyone who loved him. Help my team and me bring his killers to justice. And forgive me for every unkind, unjust and negative thought I ever harbored for him. Cleanse my heart, Lord.

Praying helped, and already her footsteps felt lighter as she saw the motel come back into view, with its rusted metal balconies and uniform orange doors.

She'd admired Lex's loyalty to his friends. Even when helping a friend whose ex had tossed all his belongings out on the lawn in a snowstorm had kept him from making it to their cake tasting or when the check for the reception venue had almost bounced because he'd bailed a friend out. It had been a really attractive quality of Lex's, if she was honest, even when his dedication to his friends had left her to handle too much on her own. And Lex's friends had cared about him, too.

After all, Johnny must've known he was risking his life by telling Lex about the blue bear cubs. Whatever mistakes he'd made, Johnny had died trying to do the right thing.

And that is what she needed to focus on.

She found Will sitting at a picnic table in front of the motel, with his back to the table and his feet out in front of him. Scout was lying under the table, and when Poppy unclipped her K-9 partner's leash, Stormy looked up at her and woofed slightly as if asking Poppy's permission to join Scout.

She patted her side. "Go ahead. If you can fit."

Poppy chuckled slightly as the large dog scrunched herself down low enough to crawl under the table and beside Scout, who patiently moved aside to accommodate her.

Will waved a hand in greeting. "You've got about forty minutes before our team meeting if you want to unpack a bit. It's just going to be a handful of us for now and then we'll have a bigger briefing tomorrow."

Poppy would definitely get changed at least. She'd been wearing the same dirt-streaked uniform all day and knew the colonel wouldn't mind if she showed up for the team meeting out of uniform. Unpacking her stuff into that grimy-looking motel was another thing altogether. She might just leave her belongings in her suitcase.

Sitting down beside Will, she leaned back against the table and stretched her legs out.

"So, how are you feeling?" he asked. She glanced Will's way, but his gaze was fixed on the sky. "Can't imagine it's easy to suddenly come face-to-face with an old boyfriend."

"Ex-fiancé," she corrected him automatically, although she suspected he knew that and was understating it to be diplomatic.

"Didn't quite stand me up at the altar, but pretty close. He was missing in action for about all of the wedding prep. Then he accidentally leaves a pocket-dial message on my answering machine, telling someone else he's having serious second thoughts."

"Ouch," Will said.

"Yup," she said. "I called Lex when I got it and asked him point-blank if he wanted to marry me. He hemmed and hawed a bit, then admitted he wasn't feeling it, and that was that. All very nondramatic and civilized."

In fact, she suspected he was surprised at how calmly she'd taken it. And sure, maybe if she had burst into tears and begged him to stay he would've still married her, considering the way he always leaped in to save people in need. But she hadn't wanted to guilt the man she loved into spending the rest of his life with her. She'd wanted him to choose her.

"Did you know Johnny or Ripley at all before this?" Will asked after a long moment.

"Ripley, no," she said. "But I worked with Johnny briefly at Kenai Fjords National Park before he got fired for some small-scale poaching. We were never close. But Lex stayed in touch with him after that and even invited him to the wedding. If I remember correctly, Johnny gave him a really nice pocketknife as an engagement gift that Lex probably still uses."

Although she wouldn't be the slightest bit surprised if Johnny had tried to talk Lex out of marrying her.

"What was your impression of him?" Will's tone was casual, but there was something very professional and investigative about it, too, which she appreciated.

"We didn't get along," she admitted, "but he was also always incredibly polite and respectful to me. He told me once that he'd take a bullet for Lex and that as 'Lex's other half' that was true for me, too." Huh, she'd completely forgotten that until now. Maybe her prayer really was working on her heart. "I think I was too irritated at being called Lex's 'other half' to realize what a big gesture that probably was for him. You know he had a criminal record?"

"Yup," Will said. "Long but petty. Selling cigarettes to people under twenty-one. Driving away from the gas station without paying…"

"Poaching small game," she added, "and hustling tourists at darts and pool. What's your impression of Ripley?"

"Her statement was all over the place, and her timeline doesn't add up," Will said. "But that's not unheard of. My impression is she's very upset and very, very scared. I wouldn't be surprised if it turns out someone was after her and Johnny, and it he boobytrapped his own property. But that's just a guess. Ripley lives with her brother, Nolan. We spoke very briefly when he came to pick her up."

"Lex implied her ex-boyfriend is a nasty piece of work," Poppy offered. "Maybe they were afraid he'd come here and go after her or Johnny."

"Interesting," Will mused. "Now that's worth looking into."

"What's your take on Ripley's brother?" she asked. "Johnny was doing mechanic work for his airline tours business."

"Honestly," Will said, "I wouldn't knock on his door without a warrant. Nolan strikes me as the kind of guy who'd shoot a trespasser first and *then* try to figure out who they were. Condition of his truck implies financial troubles, too." He shrugged. "I was kind of surprised when it turned out he didn't have a criminal record. But maybe there's something there that didn't turn up in a cursory search. He is very protective of his sister and they clearly love each other. Nolan will keep her safe."

Poppy stood and turned to head up to her room. Stormy looked up at her and her eyebrows rose hopefully, as if to say she'd join her if she had to but was hoping Poppy would let her stay with Scout. Poppy chuckled.

"Mind if Stormy hangs out with Scout while I get changed?" she asked.

"No problem," Will said. "Happy to supervise a K-9 playdate. There's a water bowl and hose around the side of the building. I'll make sure she gets something to drink."

Poppy leaned down and ran her hand over Stormy's shaggy head. "Thanks."

Half an hour later, Poppy was no closer to being unpacked, but had changed into her favorite pair of yoga pants and a soft gray T-shirt, with a sweatshirt tied around her waist just in case the temperature dropped. Her long auburn hair, which thankfully had settled from the flaming red of her youth to a color much closer to actual poppies as she'd grown older, now lay damp around her shoulders.

She knocked on the door adjoining her room to Will's.

"It's open," he called.

She slipped through into what the motel had optimistically called the "living room area" of the adjoining "suite." Will sat on the room's only chair in front of a metal folding table with his laptop open in front of him, and Stormy and Scout were curled up nearby on the stained and faded carpet. The room smelled heavily of other people's meals and pets. Will rose to offer her the chair, but she waved him down and instead perched on the arm of the couch behind him. Lex's mother's beautiful and well-maintained bed-and-breakfast brushed the edges of her mind, along with the fact Poppy had turned down Gillian's kind suggestion they all stay there, for fear of being too emotionally compromised by Lex and his adorable son, Danny. She reached her hand down toward Stormy, who licked her fingertips in welcome.

Will pressed a button and a tapestry of faces began to appear in front of them in boxes on the screen. First was her boss, Lorenza, sitting in her office with her senior K-9 husky, Denali, watching the meeting from a dog bed behind her. Poppy had always secretly thought there was something slightly glamorous about her no-nonsense boss, and tonight the pale blue scarf that wrapped around her shoulders and seemed to perfectly offset her silver pixie cut was no exception. Then came troopers Maya Rodriguez and Helena Maddox, who it seemed had gone home for the day and each called in from their respective kitchens. Then finally resident tech guru Eli Partridge, who was still at his desk, his mop of dark brown hair even more unruly than usual.

As happy as she was to see her team members, their images all seemed a bit fuzzier than usual.

"Hey, all." Eli waved at the screen and pushed his glasses up higher on his nose. "I've got most of you all coming through nice and clear. But Will and Poppy's internet connection is really weak. I was hoping to send through some detailed maps and images tomorrow morning I managed to download from a dark web illegal animal auction site that might relate to our bear poaching case, but that'll depend on them getting a better internet connection or us finding a workaround. Anyone else joining us this evening?"

"No, given the late hour I thought we'd just meet as a partial team tonight to go over a potential new development in our missing bride case," Lorenza said, "and have a larger team meeting tomorrow morning at nine."

Poppy met Maya's eyes through the screen. The two troopers had recently worked closely with their colleague, Trooper Hunter McCord, on the troubling and mysterious unsolved case of what had happened to a wedding party who'd gone hiking in the snow-covered trees of Chugach State Park. The tour guide, Cal Brooks, had been found murdered, the maid of honor, Ariel Potter, had been pushed over a cliff and almost died and the pregnant bride, Violet James, was now on the run. Maya and her Malinois, Sarge, had been part of the search party that had found the would-be-groom, Lance Wells, and best man, Jared Dennis. Both men had been pretty banged up and told Maya that Violet had knocked Lance out and shot Jared. Lance also told them that Violet was pregnant with Cal's child, but Ariel, who was now happily engaged to Hunter, was convinced her missing friend was innocent.

"Helena is planning to interview Lance's sister, Tessa, tomorrow," Lorenza said. "I understand you tried to talk to her when you spoke with Lance's parents?"

"I did." Poppy nodded. "But she was out of the country."

It had disappointed her not to be able to interview Lance's sister, especially as Lance's ex-girlfriend had suggested she might be a good person to talk to.

"I've gone over your notes from your other interviews," Helena said. "But I'd appreciate your gut perspective before I talk to her."

Her K-9 partner, Luna, leaned her head on the table beside Helena as if she was interested in hearing Poppy's perspective, too. Helena rubbed her fingers along the Norwegian elkhound's head.

"Lance's parents are definitely looking at their son through rose-colored glasses," Poppy said. "They kept telling me how wonderful he was. I got the impression they thought he could do no wrong." Again, she was thankful she'd taken the time to pray about her current case and ask God to cleanse her of anything clouding her own judgment. "His ex-girlfriend had a much less rosy opinion. She wouldn't tell me what had gone on between her and Lance, only that he'd broken things off when she didn't get an inheritance she was expecting and that she'd caught him lying too many times."

Helena's green eyes widened. "About what?"

"I don't know," Poppy said. "She said they were little white lies mostly. Nothing too serious. But she did tell me we should speak to Lance's sister."

And while she wished she'd been able to interview Tessa herself, she had every confidence that Helena would do an excellent job.

"Say we do determine that Lance isn't that great a guy," Will said. "It takes more than having a lousy personality to prove murder. After all, there are far easier ways to get out of marrying a bridezilla than killing people."

She was sure he meant it as an offhand comment. But Poppy felt her back stiffen just the same.

"A bride accused of being pregnant with another man's child," Maya pointed out.

"Thankfully that brings us to our second break in the case, which is something far more tangible than romantic intrigue," Lorenza added. "Do you want to fill them in, Maya?"

Maya nodded. "Sarge and I found an expensive gold watch belonging to our best man, Jared, at the bottom of the cliff where Ariel was pushed," she said.

Will whistled under his breath. "Well done, Sarge."

Poppy heard Maya's Malinois partner woof off-screen as if in agreement.

"The watch was a gift to him from Lance," Maya added. "He says he lost it."

"But Tala is running forensics on it to see if there's any evidence he was the one who pushed Ariel," Eli added.

And if anyone could find an evidentiary needle in a haystack, forensic scientist Tala Ekho could.

Poppy and Will filled the team in on the poaching case so far, including Johnny's death and Ripley's forcible confinement. Lorenza suggested they reinterview Ripley and also her brother tomorrow, with a special focus on the possible ex-boyfriend angle, and see if any other patrons of the unlicensed "watering hole" had heard anything about the blue bears or poaching. Eli said he'd run a search online for any information he could find out about the sale of the animals.

"One more question," Lorenza said, fixing her eyes on Poppy and Will. "Do you think Johnny told the poacher that he'd tipped Lex off to their plans before he killed him?"

"Yes," Will said automatically.

·"No," Poppy declared, just as fast, their voices speaking over each other.

"Interesting," Lorenza said. She leaned back in her chair and looked at the two of them a long moment. She nodded to Will. "Why do you say yes?"

"Looks like death was pretty quick and painless," Will explained. He glanced at Poppy almost apologetically. "There was no sign of serious injuries or that he was really hurt in any way. Which to me implies he cooperated and told them everything they wanted to know."

Lorenza nodded slowly over steepled fingers. Then she gestured at Poppy. "And why do you think Johnny didn't give Lex up?"

Because I just do.

"Hard to explain," Poppy admitted. "But Lex is the kind of man who instills loyalty among those who care about him. Despite their problems, Johnny told me that he loved Lex like a brother and would be willing to take a bullet for him. And to be honest, I believed him. Johnny risked his life to tell Lex about the poachers when he could've just protected himself and kept quiet about it. That has to mean something."

Did it? Or was that just wishful thinking

on her part? She pressed her lips together and prayed for wisdom.

"Considering the number of tranquilizer dart traps in the house, and how peacefully Johnny seemed slumped in the chair, I think we should look for evidence that Johnny was tranquilized and out cold when he was killed," she added. Then she glanced at Will. "Although I admit that wouldn't be conclusive either way about which one of us is right."

"It's also possible his kidnapper was interrupted or in a hurry," Will offered, "or that he had some other kind of personal connection to him. We can't jump to conclusions. My hunch could very well be wrong."

"As could mine," Poppy admitted.

A Bible verse from Proverbs 27 sprung suddenly to her mind about how one friend sharpens another like iron sharpens iron. Once again, she found herself thanking God for her team and how working with them strengthened her and made her a better person. Living in a place like Gustavus, cut off from the world, might work for some, but she couldn't imagine ever making that choice. And not just because it would mean giving up being part of the Alaska state trooper's K-9 unit.

After the team said their goodbyes, Poppy took Stormy for a run. Will had offered to come with her if she'd feel more comfortable with company. And she appreciated it, just like she'd appreciated the fact he hadn't pried into her past with Lex. But Scout couldn't begin to keep up with Stormy's speed, and truth was she needed time alone to think. Her footsteps pounded beneath her in a slow and steady jog, with Stormy by her side, the dog grinning at her at intervals as if she was encouraging Poppy to go faster. Every now and then, when the coast was clear of vehicles and homes, Poppy would give her permission to run and then watch as Stormy galloped off into the distance at full tilt, before always inevitably coming right back to her side like a boomerang. If there was a limit to Stormy's seemingly boundless energy, she hadn't found it yet.

Poppy had always enjoyed running, especially at the end of a long workday. She and Lex used to run together at night, and each said exercising together had somehow pushed them to be faster and train harder. Running alone had also helped a lot in those days after Lex had broken her heart. It had given her a way to work through the pain of losing him, pray and cry alone when no one was around to witness it and get her life back on track. And she'd rebuilt her life so much better than she could've ever imagined. First Lorenza had welcomed her into the incredible K-9 team. Then Stormy had tumbled into her orbit like a gigantic, overgrown puppy, so eager to learn and diligent in her training. She couldn't have asked for a better partner.

Thank You, Lord, for the team meeting tonight. It felt good to be reminded of who I am, where I belong and all You've given me. Help us stop those poachers before the second bear cub is captured and the first bear cub is sold. And please bring Johnny's killer to justice.

She hadn't even realized how far she'd run until she saw the beautiful wooden frame of Gillian's bed-and-breakfast looming ahead of her in the darkness. A light was on in the upper floor, over the covered porch, glowing like a lighthouse in the darkness. Instinctively she looked up and saw Lex, silhouetted against the gentle light of what looked like blue-and-white star-shaped wall lamps. She watched as he scooped little Danny up into his arms and spun him around, before cradling the toddler to his chest. It looked like they were laughing.

Poppy looked away as an old familiar ache filled her chest. She'd always been the kind of person who made plans and set goals—and the one dashed dream that had hurt most of all was when Lex had decided he didn't want to have a family with her. She'd always longed to be a wife and mother every bit as strongly as she'd desired her career. And while she didn't resent Lex his happiness, it hurt to be reminded that he'd rejected her and created that family with someone else. Thick drops of rain brushed her skin and thunder rumbled, warning her of the storm that was to come. She stopped and glanced at her watch, surprised to realize it was already eight. Stormy whined softly as if asking to keep going.

"I don't have another sprint in me," Poppy told the dog. "But if you want one last run before we turn around, go for it. I'll wait here for you."

She ran her hand over Stormy's head, then patted her side. The K-9 woofed and bounded off into the darkness. Poppy sat down on a stump, with her back against a fence post and Lex's window out of view. She had pushed herself too far and now would have a long walk back in the rain for her troubles, along with sharing an underwhelming motel room with a huge and soaking-wet shaggy dog.

Lord, help me focus on the task ahead of me and keep my own broken heart from getting in the way.

A motion drew her attention to the bushes at her right. For a moment, she thought it was a wild animal or even her own partner trying to sneak up on her playfully.

She stood slowly and saw the figure of a man half-hidden in the darkness, his masked face staring up at the same window where Lex and his son now stood. The light of a cell phone camera glowed in his hand.

He was filming them.

"Hey!" she shouted, leaping from behind the relative coverage of the bushes, her hand instinctively reaching for the weapon she'd left locked in her motel room. "Stop!"

The masked man turned toward her and snarled. He pocketed the phone, then a knife glinted in his grasp. He leaped at her.

SIX

The sound of a crash outside yanked Lex's attention to the window.

"Bear, Daddy?" Danny asked cheerfully. "Fox?"

He had yet to convince his small son that the parade of wild animals that tried to take up residence in their backyard, including moose, caribou and plain old raccoons, wasn't necessarily a good thing.

"Probably," Lex said, keeping his voice light, despite the warning chill that nudged his spine. He set the boy back down on his bed and raised the toddler safety rails. "I'm going to go check on the animal and come right back to read you a story. Can you pick one out for me?"

"Uh-huh." The toddler nodded enthusiastically.

Lex brushed a kiss over the boy's head and

turned. His mother was standing in the doorway. Worry filled her eyes, and he knew without needing to ask she'd heard the noise, too.

"Stay here with him," he said softly. "I'm going to check it out."

He ran down the stairs, taking them two at a time and praying with each step. He burst outside, the house's motion sensor lights flickering on to greet him. Light washed over the lawn to the edges of the road and then he saw them. Two figures were rolling and fighting on the ground, locked in a battle for dominance. A thin masked figure in camouflage was on top, trying in vain to stab the other as she dodged his blows and kicked back furiously.

His heart stopped. It was Poppy. Lex pelted across the grass toward them. The masked figure turned and Poppy struck, catching her attacker hard in the jaw with both feet. He flew back and scrambled down the road into the darkness.

"Poppy!" Lex reached her side, his arms stretched out for her as she grabbed hold of them and pulled herself up. "What's going on? Are you okay?"

"He…he was spying on you and your son." Her words came out in short, breathless gasps.

An engine sounded, cutting off their words, and he looked up to see a dark van peeling away with the masked figure at the wheel.

For a moment he felt Poppy almost wilt into his arms as if her legs had crumpled beneath her. Then she stepped back and tossed her hair out around her shoulders.

Footsteps sounded like something galloping toward them through the darkness. Instinctively, Lex took a farther step back and raised his hands palm up as Stormy burst through the trees.

"Stormy," Poppy called. "At ease. Everything's okay."

The wolfhound skidded to a stop at Poppy's feet, dropping into a sit. She looked up at Lex, her large tail thumping the ground and her jaw hanging open in a wide grin. So, no hard feelings, then.

"What are you both doing here?" he asked.

"Just getting some exercise before bed," Poppy said. "Didn't realize how far we'd come when we'd hit the bed-and-breakfast. Turns out Gustavus is a pretty small town." She ran her hand over the dog's head. "I stopped to turn around and let Stormy get in a final sprint off-leash when I saw the masked man in fatigues watching you and Danny through the window. I think he was filming you or maybe taking pictures."

The chill that had brushed Lex's spine when he'd heard the noise outside grew colder. First Gillian had seen someone watching Danny over the fence, now this. He reached out for Poppy, somehow wanting the comfort of her hand, but she stepped away from his touch, leaving him unsure if she even noticed.

"Well, I'm glad really you're here," he said. As if on cue, the intermittent drops of rain that had been falling around them broke through the clouds into a full-fledged deluge. He waved his hand toward the house. "Come on. I've got to finish putting Danny to bed, then we can talk and I'll drive you back."

Her chin rose. "It's okay, we can walk."

Yup, Poppy could walk for over half an hour, alone, at night, through the pouring rain, right after battling a masked stranger. Wouldn't surprise him in the slightest if she did.

"I don't doubt you can," he said. "But I'd feel better if you didn't. We need to talk, you need to contact your partner and I'd rather get out of the rain."

He started toward the house, thankful when she and Stormy followed.

"Yeah, you're right," she said. "We should debrief, and we didn't really get much of a chance to talk as the scene wrapped up at Johnny's house. I thought we'd wait until tomorrow, but under the circumstances, we should probably do it sooner than later."

"Absolutely," he replied. "We should talk."

But there was more to it than that. Part of him also just wanted to protect her, to have her close and know she was safe. Was that wrong? They crossed the yard and entered the house. He closed the front door, and for the first time he could remember since moving to Gustavus, he locked it behind him.

"I've got a fire going in the fireplace," he added. "Feel free to sit and dry off a bit. All of the sweatshirts hanging on the pegs by the door are clean if you want to borrow one and change into something dry. And you're welcome to join Danny and me upstairs for story time, if you want."

"Thank you," Poppy said, and as she met his eyes something seemed to hover unspoken in the air between them.

Looking back on his time with her, Lex had never quite been able to believe that someone as beautiful, smart and all around incredible as her had ever been in his life.

Now here she was, standing just two feet inside the threshold of his own home, somehow even more amazing in every way than he'd allowed himself to remember. While he had no idea where they even belonged in each other's lives, Poppy had been the one person he'd been close to who he'd never felt needed him. Sure, she might've loved him every bit as fiercely as he'd loved her, but he'd never doubted that she'd do just fine without him. And she had.

"Make yourself comfortable," he told her. "My home is yours."

Suddenly, it was like he was struck by the full weight of just how much he'd missed her. He longed to gather her close and hold her against his chest as he promised to care for and protect her.

And then he wanted to raise her face to his and kiss her lips.

Instead, he wrenched his gaze away from hers and headed up the stairs to his son, as the weight of everything he'd lost beat down against his heart.

Poppy stood and watched as Lex disappeared up the stairs to the second floor. Part of her wanted to follow him. Instead, she turned and walked into the large living area to her right and paced the space a moment to settle her mind before calling Will. The bed-and-breakfast was an open concept, with huge wood-beamed ceilings. Several smaller living areas were set off by clusters of couches, soft chairs and low tables, with shelves that Lex had made from reclaimed wood that she recognized from his old apartment in Anchorage. A wide kitchen lay to the right of the room, separated from the living area by a marble-topped island and a wooden dining table set for six that looked like it could be expanded to sit double that. Behind the kitchen led a hallway to what seemed to be several guest rooms and a second staircase by the side door leading back upstairs. Framed cross-stitched Bible verses and pictures of Lex, Gillian and little Danny were everywhere.

At some point, Stormy stopped following her, and when Poppy returned to the main living area she found her K-9 partner stretched out in front of a fireplace. The same tiny calico kitten she'd seen in the window earlier now weaved in and out between the wolfhound's giant paws as if looking for a place to settle. Stormy looked up at Poppy under shaggy brows.

"Looks like you've made a friend," she said. The kitten curled up beside Stormy's snout and closed its eyes with a purr far louder than Poppy would've imagined a tiny ball of fluff that small could've mustered. She laughed softly.

"And good for you," she told the kitten, "for being so brave and gutsy to befriend someone a hundred times your size. I like you."

Even if she was feeling anything but brave herself when it came to her own relationship with Lex. She untied her damp sweatshirt from around her waist and rubbed it over her head like a towel. She glanced at herself in the wood-framed mirror over the mantel. Her own wide eyes stared back at her, looking twice as large as usual in her pale face. The youthful flush on her cheeks and unfamiliar fluttering in her chest seemed to belong to a woman who'd lived half the years and heartaches she had. She pulled a dark green zip-up sweatshirt from the pegs by the door, put it on and zipped it up. The achingly familiar scent of Lex filled her senses.

She called Will and he answered on the first ring.

"Everything okay?" he asked. "You've been gone awhile."

After Poppy quickly filled him in on the details of what had happened, he blew out a hard breath.

"Gotta say I'm getting tired of being in a place this far away from law enforcement backup," he said. "I'll make a preliminary report to the team, and you can fill in more details when you're back at your laptop. You want me to come pick you up?"

"Probably in a bit," she replied. "I need to talk to Lex first. He's busy putting his son to bed."

"Call anytime," Will said. "I don't mind if you wake me up."

"Thank you. I really appreciate it."

"And hey," he added. "I'm really sorry if I came down too hard on your point of view or anything in the team meeting earlier."

"Don't be and you didn't," she said. "I really like that we have different opinions. It makes us both better at our jobs."

"Okay, good." Will sighed. "I also felt kind of bad about that offhand comment I made about there being easier ways to get out of a wedding than killing someone. I mean, I had my heart broken once by someone I loved and I know it's no joking matter. I might not be the biggest on opening up about personal stuff, but if you need a friend you can always talk to me."

"Thank you," she said again, feeling a smile spread across her face. "To be honest, I'd completely forgotten you'd said that and I'm trying to keep my personal feelings out of the case right now. But I'm really glad to know that if anything does come up I can talk to you."

"Good," Will replied, and she could hear the smile in his voice. "Hopefully we'll wrap this mess up soon and get back to Anchorage, where you've got a whole team of people who've got your back, too."

Yeah, it had been good to see some of their faces on the video call earlier and she looked forward to seeing even more of them in the morning.

"Thanks for the reminder," she said.

"Anytime."

The call ended and she glanced at Stormy, who was now snoring softly, still cuddling with her new kitten friend. She left them there asleep and started up the stairs to the second floor. Lex's and Danny's voices wafted down the hallway toward her, and she followed them to the toddler's room. The door was ajar, and she stopped a few paces away from it and listened. By the sound of things Lex was reading a story about a very silly pigeon who kept asking for things he couldn't have. Lex was playing the role of the pigeon in a cartoonish voice while Danny kept telling the pigeon no, in between gales of hysterical giggles.

Her breath caught. The happiness and love that flowed between father and son was so obvious. And the weight of all the times she'd tried and failed to convince Lex that he'd be a good father crashed down around her heart, sending unshed tears to her eyes. She closed them tightly and stopped the tears from falling.

Help me, Lord... I don't want to be jealous or resentful of Lex's happiness. I want to be happy for him. I don't want to feel this sadness in my heart. Please erase my pain so it doesn't impact my actions now.

"Keep go'n, Daddy!" Danny squealed. "More pi'gon!"

She turned and started down the stairs, back to the living room, where she sat on a couch and tried to distract herself with a Victorian suspense novel she found on a side table. Stormy had rearranged herself into a giant circle on the floor, tucking her nose against her tail, and the kitten had curled itself into a new ball inside it. Ten minutes later, she heard Lex's footsteps on the stairs, but didn't look up until she heard his voice.

"Hey, how are you doing?" he asked softly. He sat down on the opposite end of the couch and turned toward her, leaning his back against the arm.

"I'm okay," she said. "How about you?"

He ran his hand over his neck.

"Tired," he admitted. He glanced at Stormy and the kitten, and chuckled. "So looks like someone didn't get the memo about Stormy being a big scary beast."

"What's the kitten's name?" she asked. "I've been talking to it on and off and felt bad I didn't know what to call it."

"His name is Mushroom," Lex said. A grin crossed his face, as if happy for the brief distraction from more serious topics. "Danny named him, although he pronounces it Mu'shoom. It's apparently short for Mushroom Pizza."

Poppy snorted, barely catching the laugh in her hand as it spilled out over her fingers.

"That's a great name for a kitten," she said.

"I agree." Lex's smile grew wider. "I think it's because of the calico pattern, but I'm not quite sure."

And for a long moment they sat there, neither of them saying anything, just listening to the sound of the rain beating against the window and the fire crackling in the hearth. She turned to face him and leaned back against the opposite arm of the chair. Their knees bumped.

"I called Will and briefed him," she said. "We had a short team meeting tonight and will have another longer one tomorrow with the entire team."

"Your entire team is participating in a joint meeting about Johnny's murder and the poaching of blue bear cubs?" he asked.

"Yes and no," she replied. "We try to have regular team meetings with the K-9 unit about the various cases we're working on. We have three main ongoing investigations right now, along with this one."

"What are the other cases?" he asked.

For a moment she wondered if he was just making small talk, until she saw the keen interest shining in his eyes.

"Well, one that's right up your alley is

what's been happening at the Family K Reindeer Sanctuary Ranch," she said.

"That's the one run by Addie Kapowski?"

She wasn't surprised he was familiar with it. Lex had always had a close relationship with the various animal sanctuaries around Anchorage.

"Yup," she said. "Addie's niece, Katie, is my boss Lorenza's assistant. A pen of reindeer were let loose recently and all but two were accounted for. Stormy and I were part of the team that found one of them, but the other one is still missing and we can't discount the possibility it was stolen and whoever poached it will be back for more."

Lex frowned. "If there's anything I can do to help with that, let me know."

"Thanks," she said. "I'm sure my team will appreciate that. Also, I'm looking forward to hearing from my colleagues Sean and Gabriel, who are currently searching Chugach State Park for a family of survivalists named the Seavers. The father of the family is the son of our tech guru Eli's godmother. She's dying of cancer and hoping to reconcile with them before it's too late."

"Chugach State Park is also where a bride recently went missing, right?" Lex asked.

Considering the case had made national news she shouldn't be too shocked it reached Gustavus.

"Violet James, yes," she said. "I've been working that case, too."

"Did they ever find any of them? I haven't really followed the case."

"The tour guide, Cal Brooks, was found murdered," she informed him. "The maid of honor, Ariel Potter, was found at the bottom of a cliff with nonfatal injuries. She helped us find the missing reindeer actually and is now engaged to my colleague Hunter McCord. I really like her. The groom, Lance Wells, and the best man, Jared Dennis, were found holed up in a cabin and severely injured. Lance had been hit over the head and Jared was shot. They say it was Violet."

"Who is still missing," Lex confirmed.

"Who is pregnant and believed to be on the run," Poppy said. "Lance claims she was having an affair with the dead tour guide and the baby is Cal's. I'm suspicious of Lance, though, after the mixed messages I got from my interviews and not sure he can be trusted." Then she found Will's words leaving her lips. "After all, there are far easier ways to get out of marrying a bridezilla than trying to kill them."

It was a throwaway line, something meaningless, and she wasn't even sure why she'd said it.

But Lex leaned toward her and grabbed her hands.

"You don't think that's what happened with us, right?" he asked thickly.

"Not really, no," she said, "although I had gotten very caught up in wedding planning—"

"Because you were incredibly organized," Lex interjected. "You were good at all that wedding stuff so I just left you to it."

"I didn't want you to leave me to it." Poppy stood, pulling her hands out of his grasp. Was that what he thought? "I wanted us to work together. I wanted us to be partners. But you said it yourself, just hours ago, that we were never good at being a team. It was like you never wanted to listen when I talked about wedding plans, and every time I made an appointment for something important you canceled on me because somebody else needed you more."

He leaped to his feet, too, and for a long moment they just stood there, face-to-face, just a breath away from each other, and neither of them stepped back.

"I don't understand," Lex said. "You think I called off marrying you because I didn't want to help you with wedding planning?"

"No, of course not," Poppy protested. "I didn't know what to think. How could I? You didn't explain. You just told me you weren't ready to be a husband or father."

"I told you I was having doubts," Lex said. "I was very honest about that."

"But you never explained why you were having doubts about me…or what I could do about it."

"Because I wasn't having doubts about you!" Lex burst out. "You might be the most dedicated and driven person I've ever met in my life, but you still can't fix something that's not your doing. I didn't have a single doubt that you were an incredible, amazing, beautiful woman and any man would give his right arm to be married to you." His voice dropped, his tone growing huskier. "I doubted that I could be what you needed and that I had what it took to be the kind of man you deserved."

Poppy's heart seemed to gasp, sending shivers coursing through her veins. A moment later, she took a deep, fortifying breath and forced herself to have the courage to say the words she needed to say. "Then you went and had a family with somebody else."

"Do you think I was the same man when I had Danny that I was when I gave up on us?" he asked. "Because I wasn't. Losing you broke me into pieces. It destroyed me, blew my life apart, made me reexamine my life and, with God's help, reshaped me into being someone better than I'd ever been before." He stepped closer and their fingertips touched. "Losing you changed me, irrevocably."

"It changed me, too," she whispered.

Thunder crashed outside the window. She looked up into his handsome face and watched as something softened in the depths of his eyes. His mouth opened, and then closed again, as if his brain kept coming up with words he wouldn't let himself speak. Finally, he said, "I'm sorry if I ever made you doubt how much I wanted you to be my wife."

His fingers brushed up her arm until they rested on her cheek. Her hands slid up his back. And they both stood there for a long moment, frozen in a tableau, and Poppy feeling somehow both lost and found at once.

"What are you thinking?" she asked.

Lex broke his gaze as a wistful grin turned at one corner of his mouth. "Honestly?"

"Yes, honestly," she said.

His eyes met hers again. "I'm thinking I missed you."

SEVEN

"I missed you, too," Poppy admitted softly. Then she felt her eyes close as Lex pulled her closer into his chest. Her face tilted up toward his.

"Lex!" Gillian's voice sounded from somewhere behind them as footsteps clattered on the stairs.

She opened her eyes and leaped back, feeling Lex pull away from her equally as fast. They turned and she watched as the older woman appeared in the doorway. And Poppy wasn't sure if she'd just arrived on the main floor, or if she'd seen their embrace and then stepped back and announced her presence to be polite. The cheerful smile that crossed Gillian's face as she entered the room gave nothing away.

"Actually, I was looking for you, Poppy," she said. "I wanted to ask you again if you and your colleague would consider relocating here for your time in Gustavus. We have two large suites on the main floor that would have plenty of room for your K-9 partners. You'd have full use of the kitchen and the fenced-in backyard. And as we don't open again for the season for a few days yet, you'd be free to use our common areas for your meetings. We've also got high-speed internet, plus a photo-quality color printer and fax machine if you need it."

The idea of getting out of the motel was even more appealing now after she'd spent a bit more time there and Eli had said the motel's internet wasn't up to the task for what he needed for the meeting tomorrow. As much as she'd enjoyed taking Stormy for a walk, it was no substitute to having an actual yard she could play in.

"I'll be honest," Gillian added. "I'd feel safer with you here. It's twice in one day we've had a prowler outside our home watching my grandson. And as you know, we don't have an active police force in Gustavus. If you need, I can call your boss and formally request your protection."

"I'm sure she'll agree," Poppy said, "and

as for Will, he'll be thrilled to move him and Scout here. Thank you."

In fact, there was no good reason to stay in the motel when they could relocate the operation here. None except the fact she suspected the man who'd once broken her heart had been about to kiss her, and she'd been on the verge of kissing him, too.

Thankfully calling Will gave her an excuse to walk away from the confusing moment she'd almost had with Lex and the distraction of something else to think about.

Within moments her colleague had agreed to relocate. While the continued threat against Lex's son and the realization they'd be better equipped to do their jobs and coordinate with their team from the bed-and-breakfast definitely played into it, she was sure part of him was just happy to be out of the underwhelming surroundings. Since she hadn't unpacked her suitcase yet and had even left it zipped, Will was happy to grab her stuff and bring it over with him and Scout.

Less than half an hour later, he had arrived, and Gillian was showing Poppy to her new digs. The room had high ceilings, with an ensuite bathroom and a large colorful rug more than big enough for Stormy to stretch out on at the end of the large four-poster bed. Lex was standing in the living room with Will as she said a quick good-night to them both, without quite meeting Lex's eye. Then she lay awake, willing her body to sleep and reminding herself of all the reasons why this relocation made the most logical sense, despite what her heart might feel.

She awoke to sun streaming through the window, the scent of coffee, eggs and bacon wafting down the hall from the kitchen and the gentle whine of Stormy standing politely by the bed. The wolfhound's head plonked down on the pillow beside Poppy's at eye level. She rolled over and rubbed Stormy between the ears. Then she got up, got dressed and steeled herself to face whatever the day held.

When she stepped out into the hallway and headed for the living area, a cacophony of ridiculous and happy noises reached her ears, including what sounded like giggling, howling and high-pitched music wailing. What was she listening to? She rounded the corner as Stormy galloped in one step ahead of her, and saw Danny sitting alone in a high chair at the kitchen table facing Will's laptop and laughing wildly.

A few more steps into the room revealed Will was standing by the counter, fixing himself coffee, and Lex was at the stove making scrambled eggs. Each was keeping a watchful eye on whatever Danny was doing.

The tall and blond form of Trooper Sean West sat at a desk, attempting what sounded like "Twinkle Twinkle Little Star" on a harmonica while his K-9 partner, an Akita named Grace, was sing slash howling along. Danny was a rapt audience, oscillating between trying to sing and dissolving into giggles.

Sean's eye met hers through the screen and he grinned.

She waved and he waved back.

"Hey, Poppy!" Sean said. "Sorry, been having a lot of time alone in remote areas recently and been trying to teach myself something new. Still need a lot of practice."

She laughed.

"It's great," she said. "Don't stop on my account."

Her colleague's grin widened.

"Are you good with starting our team meeting in fifteen or twenty?" Sean asked.

She glanced around the kitchen. An array of cereal, bagels, bacon and fruit spread across the kitchen counter, along with the scrambled eggs Lex was fixing.

"No problem," she said.

"Great, I'll let the others know," Sean said. He pushed a button and his face disappeared.

She turned and looked quizzically at Will.

"Am I late?" she asked.

"Sean's early," Will said. "He and Gabriel had a lead he wanted to chase, so he called hoping that we could bump up the call time."

"Big doggy sing, too?" Danny's hopeful voice drew her gaze back to where the toddler sat in his high chair pushing cereal around on the table.

"She doesn't sing," Poppy told him. "But she barks and howls, very loudly."

Danny's little face fell.

"But she does other tricks. Do you want to see?"

The little boy's eyes widened again as he nodded. Wordlessly Lex took the skillet of eggs off the heat, turned the stove off, fixed a cup of coffee and came around the other side of the island to join his son. She hadn't even realized that he'd fixed the coffee for her until he offered it to her and asked, "Half a spoonful of sugar, two splashes of milk, right?"

He'd remembered.

"Perfect," she said. "Thank you."

He set it down on the table in front of her. She picked it up, took a long sip, then called Stormy over to her side, oddly feeling the same nervous flutter in her chest of not wanting to let her audience down that she'd felt when demonstrating Stormy's training to Lorenza.

Immediately, the wolfhound left the ray of sun by the sliding door where she'd been chilling with Scout, walked over and stood in front of her expectedly. Poppy did a quick mental calculation. Standing, the dog's face was almost parallel with her shoulder, and despite the fact the ceiling was probably nine feet, showing off how high the dog could leap was probably best left as an outside trick.

"Okay," she said, "I'm going to give Stormy some instructions and you copy what I do, okay?"

Danny's smile lit his face. "'Kay!"

She slowly walked Stormy through sitting, lying down, rolling and crawling, while Lex helped Danny follow along with the gestures and commands. Gillian appeared in the doorway partway through the demonstration and stood there watching the show. Danny's favorite trick was definitely watching the huge dog sneakily crawling across the floor like a secret agent and had her demonstrate it three times, before Lex challenged Stormy to see which one of them could crawl the quietest and most stealthily. The dog won. Finally, she took her K-9 partner's favorite ball and hid it behind the bookshelf while Danny covered the dog's eyes with her ears. Stormy dutifully weaved her way around the room sniffing, before sitting in front of the shelf and woofing triumphantly. Danny clapped and cheered.

His grandmother scooped him up into his arms. "Come on, little man. You need to get ready for preschool. I'll be staying as a special helper with you today, too."

Danny waved goodbye to Stormy as he left. The dog trotted to the sliding door and barked hopefully. Poppy let him and Scout out, not even realizing Mushroom had joined them, too, until she skittered past her ankles. She watched for a moment as the three animals jumped and pounced in the air around each other in some elaborate game the three of them all seemed to understand, then she went and helped herself to breakfast.

Ten minutes later, Poppy sat at the kitchen table beside Will, who made a big show of pointing out just how many chair options there were compared to their meeting in the dingy motel the night before. As the team video call reloaded, she could see Lex in the screen's reflection behind them. He was standing at the counter, as if waiting to see if he should go, despite the fact Will had asked him to stay for now. Between Gillian, Danny and Will, she and Lex hadn't been alone in the room once since their awkward moment the night before.

Lord, help me just focus on my job today.

The video call started, and boxes popped up around the screen with Lorenza, Eli and Maya, now joined by Sean, Gabriel Runyon and Brayden Ford, with various K-9 partners wandering in and out of the shots for pats and to wag their tails at the screen. The only two team members absent were Helena and Hunter. Helena was off interviewing Lance's sister, Tessa, as she'd mentioned the night before. And Hunter was taking some well-deserved time off with his new fiancée, Ariel.

"Anybody else feel like we're all in a 1980s game show when we're on one of these calls?" Eli asked, glancing around the screen. "Will and Poppy, you're coming through much clearer and sharper this morning. So, I'm going to try to load up the graphics I mentioned last night." He started typing furiously.

Lorenza waved to the group, wished everyone a good-morning and started the meeting.

"I'd like to introduce everyone to Park Ranger Lex Fielding," Will said, gesturing behind him. "I hope it's okay that I've included him in this meeting. I think he'll have some good insights on the information Eli's sending through."

"Of course." Lorenza smiled widely. "It's nice to see you again, Lex."

Again?

"I didn't realize you'd ever met," Poppy said.

She glanced at Lex in surprise, but it was Lorenza who answered.

"We met at an Alaskan trooper recruitment event some years back," she said. "As I remember, his fiancée had been encouraging him to consider a career with the troopers. We had a great talk about his skills and interests, and I recommended he stay with the park rangers, as that seemed to be where both his talents and his heart lay. Glad to see you did," she added with a smile, "because it might be good to get your input on some of this, too."

Sean and Gabriel opened by quickly running the team through their attempts to search Chugach State Park for Eli's godmother's survivalist family. Sean explained that while they'd seen no glimpse of the family itself, they had run into two hunters who looked like survivalists. When they'd asked about the Seavers, the hunters had been tightlipped and told them to mind their own business.

"They didn't exactly threaten us," Gabriel added, scratching his Saint Bernard partner, Bear, on the top of his shaggy head. "But it was also implied it would be in our own best interest to stop poking around asking questions. More troubling is that we sidestepped a few fairly nasty traps set in the forest, which we suspect were more for keeping nosy outsiders away than actual hunting."

"What kind of traps?" Lex asked. He moved forward and leaned a palm on the table beside her. "Do you think they were specifically designed for people?"

Poppy sat back and listened as her colleagues described the various traps they'd come across in detail, including trip wires, ropes and various incapacitating weapons. Lex leaned even farther toward the camera, peppering them with very specific questions and then explaining in detail how such snares were constructed and how to avoid them. Poppy could tell that Sean and Gabriel were beyond thankful. She also couldn't help but notice there was that same spark in Lorenza's eyes as she listened to Lex, that her boss got whenever she seemed to be internally celebrating seeing a member of the team excel at their work. Poppy didn't know whether she should be more surprised that Lex had actually gone to an Alaska trooper recruitment event and sought out her mentor for advice— or by the fact he hadn't told her.

As expected, there was no update on the missing bride case as they'd discussed it the night before. She gathered that forensic scientist, Tala Ekho, who wasn't on the call, presumably hadn't finished analyzing the watch that was found at the bottom of the cliff. Although Poppy knew that Lex would've quickly left the room if they had, as he was a civilian and Lorenza would've been unlikely to allow him to be briefed on the case without very good reason.

Then came Eli's briefing on the blue bear poachers.

"So, the bad news is I'm still no closer to figuring out where this black market auction is going to take place," Eli said. His mouth scrunched in a grimace "It's all very vague and encrypted. I never would've even found these posts if we hadn't known about this poaching case from Lex."

Who'd learned about it from Johnny, Poppy thought, who it seemed had lost his life because of it.

"Do we know when it's happening?" Poppy asked.

"It says the day after tomorrow," Eli said.

"Which gives them a pretty small window of time to poach the second bear cub," Poppy pointed out.

And not a lot of time for the team to stop them.

Eli nodded. "But the good news is we've now got pictures."

He clicked a button and a slideshow of images he'd pulled from the dark web postings filled the screen. There sat a blue bear cub sitting cramped and miserable in what looked like a dog carrier.

"What kind of monster would do that to a defenseless animal!" Maya exclaimed off-screen.

"Agreed!" Brayden chimed in. "First we've

got reindeer disappearing off Katie's aunt's farm and now this."

Frustration coursed through the trooper's voice like he wanted to step through the screen and rescue the cub himself. Poppy knew how he felt as she stared into the sad bear's eyes.

Lord, please help me find and rescue this poor baby and find his sibling before it's captured.

"Now they claim to have captured a male cub," Eli went on, and it sounded like he was doing his best to push his own emotional reaction at bay, "and that the other cub is female. Here they are together."

The screen clicked and a picture of two much smaller bear cubs filled the screen, with their mother in the background. The mother looked like a black bear, except for a silvery sheen of fur on her stomach and paws, but the two cubs' fur had a distinct silver-blue sheen.

"Yeah, those are definitely blue bears," Lex breathed. "Can you expand the picture at all?"

"On it," Eli said, and the picture grew to show that they were at the water's edge with what looked like a steep rock slope behind them leading up to forest beyond.

"I know where that is!" Lex declared. His

finger jabbed in the direction of the screen. "It'll take about two hours to get there, first by truck and then by boat. Although judging by the bear's size this was taken several weeks ago. Still, it's worth checking out."

"Do it," Lorenza said. Her face reappeared on the screen with the rest of the team and her gaze fixed on Poppy. "If the post's timeline is correct, we don't have much time to stop the second cub from being poached. Lex, I assume you can take her there?"

He nodded. "Absolutely."

Poppy tried not to think about the fact this meant they'd be spending more time alone. Stormy was a poacher-detection dog, and she'd spent far more time working in national parks than Will. It made perfect sense for her to be the one to go with Lex.

Still…

"Will," Lorenza continued, "I'd like you to talk to anyone you can who's connected to the watering hole where Johnny supposedly overheard this information. I want to know everyone he talked to, played pool with, threw darts with and sat next to in the past two months. We'll also see what we can pull up from this end about Ripley, her brother, Nolan, and her ex-boyfriend." She glanced to Lex. "Do you happen to know her ex-boy-friend's name?"

"Sorry, no," Lex said. He shook his head and sighed. "I hadn't really been in touch with Johnny for the past few months and he was always very private about his relationships. If anything he was the kind of guy who didn't admit he was in some kind of trouble until it was too late."

The call ended shortly afterward in a flurry of goodbyes, and while Poppy had also been hoping for an update on the missing reindeer case, she looked forward to the next time she could talk to Lorenza's assistant about it, to find out how things were on her aunt's reindeer farm.

Poppy finished her own breakfast, fed Stormy along with Scout and Mushroom, went for a quick walk with her K-9 partner and then got herself ready for the day. When she left the house and got to the truck, she found Will and Lex talking, and while they wrapped up as she approached, she couldn't shake the feeling they were talking about something seriously.

She wished Will a good day and got into the truck with Stormy, and then Lex headed out. For a long moment, he didn't say anything.

"Everything okay?" she asked eventually. "Things seemed tense with you and Will."

"They were fine," Lex said. His eyes were fixed on the road ahead. "Will just wanted to give me his condolences on Johnny's death and say that he would do everything he could to make sure the poachers were caught and Johnny's killer faced justice."

He paused for a long moment, but she had the hunch he wasn't finished. Eventually he added, "He also wanted to apologize, although I said it wasn't necessary. He said he might've been a little harsh in his assessment of Johnny yesterday, but you'd set him straight."

Now, finally, Lex glanced her way. "He said you told him that Johnny once said he'd take a bullet for me. That was really nice of you to stand up for him that way."

"No problem," she said. "I mean, we still don't know everything that happened between Johnny and the poachers. But I know he really cared about you and I don't think he'd ever knowingly hurt you or your family."

Lex looked straight ahead. "Did Johnny

ever tell you he'd take a bullet for you, too, if you married me?"

"He did," she admitted. "I told Will that, as well."

"Even though you never really liked him?" Lex asked.

"I didn't like some of the stuff he did," she admitted. "I didn't like thinking that his life was going down the drain and maybe taking you with it. I always suspected he told you not to marry me."

"Oh, he did," Lex said. "He tried to talk me out of marrying you more than once. He told me he thought I could do better and I told him he'd got that backward."

They drove through the gate to Glacier Bay National Park. Tall fir trees towered around them on both sides.

"Why didn't you tell me you'd gone to a trooper recruitment event and met my boss?" she asked quietly.

"Because nothing came of it," Lex said. "We had a long talk and she advised me to stay a park ranger—that was it."

There was more to it than that, Poppy suspected, seeing the way Lex's brow was furrowed. But she could also tell by the way he had answered the question he wasn't about to tell her more now.

They drove through the national park, and Lex stopped briefly to check in with colleagues at the ranger's station. Then they went down to a dock, where a small, white park ranger boat was docked. He climbed on board the boat, then hesitated as if he wasn't sure whether or not to reach for her hand. She and Stormy leaped on board.

Lex pulled out his phone.

"You should check for any messages now," he said, "before we get going. Once we get into the glaciers cell signal pretty much disappears. Although I do have both a satellite phone and radio for emergencies."

"Thanks." She got out her phone, checked the screen and didn't see anything out of the usual, just a few follow-up messages from the team meeting earlier.

Then she glanced at Lex. He was staring down at the phone in his hand, his fingers white and his jaw set so tightly it almost shook.

"Hey, Lex?" She stepped toward him and brushed her hand against his arm. "Everything okay?"

His eyes met hers, fury roiling in their depths.

"I just got a text," he said. "It's from a blocked number."

He held up the phone so she could read.

You saw what happened to your friend. Now you know what happens to people who try to mess with me. This is your final warning. Stay out of my business. Or your son is next.

A coldness seemed to cut through the air as the boat drove through the choppy Pacific waters that had nothing to do with the snow-capped glaciers that hemmed them on either side.

Lex had listened in as Poppy had informed the team of the threatening text and Eli had promised they'd do their best to track it. Both he and Poppy had spoken to Will and made him aware. He'd also called his mother, who'd promised she'd keep Danny surrounded by friends until Lex, Will or Poppy was able to take over watching him. They'd done all they could do. And yet, as they drove through the stunning and picturesque national park, past the roughly hewn rocks, waterfalls, endless trees and towering ice, a deep anguish settled in his heart that seemed to overshadow his ability to even see or appreciate the world around him.

Help me, Lord. First they kill Johnny. Now they threaten my son.

He glanced at the woman standing next to him, her dark red hair flying in the breeze and tickling her cheeks. She could've stayed in the lower, covered part of the boat where Stormy now dozed. But she'd chosen to stand up by the wheel beside him. Not talking or trying to draw him out in conversation, and instead just being there.

Somehow knowing that was exactly what he needed.

"What do you think of Glacier Bay?" he asked.

"It really is stunning," Poppy said. Wonder filled her voice. "No wonder you wanted to bring me here and show me all this."

Yeah, Lex thought, he really had back when he'd been planning on spending the rest of his life with her. Long before he'd decided that this very small town and huge, glacial national park was where he wanted to escape to in order to start his new life, part of him had always loved it here.

Despite himself he felt an old familiar grin curl on his lips.

"I knew you'd love it," he said.

"You were right," Poppy said. "In fact, the only thing that's stopping me from moving to a place like this myself is my job. Being based in Anchorage allows us to respond to cases all over the state quickly. Out here, we'd have to fly hours everywhere we went. It just wouldn't work."

True. Which is why he'd never even considered it until she'd been gone from his life.

She fell silent again and questions tumbled through his mind as he glanced at the beautiful woman beside him. He'd told her so much about the life he'd lived since he'd last seen her face. But he knew so little about hers. Sure, he knew about her job and could see firsthand how she'd excelled at it. He knew her last name hadn't changed; she'd never mentioned a family and didn't wear a wedding ring. But had she gone on to have any other relationships? Had she ever fallen in love again? And if so, why did the thought bother him so much when he'd clearly gone on to get married and have a family of his own?

Or was having a job she loved enough for her?

"Your team seems pretty amazing," he said.

She smiled. "They are."

"Please thank your colleague Sean for me for spending all that time with Danny," he said. "It was really kind, and Danny had so much fun talking with him."

"I will," Poppy said. "Sean's great with kids. I get the impression sometimes he wishes he had some of his own. I don't know the whole story, but he was married once and it didn't work out. His ex-wife, Ivy, grew up in a survivalist family, which is why he's taken a lead in helping us find the Seavers."

She turned and faced him, sending her hair flying down one side of her face. It was stunning. He took a deep breath.

"I'm a bit surprised you never had kids of your own," he admitted. "I thought there'd be a line of guys a mile long wanting to ask you out."

Poppy shrugged. "Well, if so, nobody told me."

Was she blind? Did she really have no idea how attractive and impressive she was?

"What about Teddy England?" Lex asked. Poppy's nose wrinkled a moment like she was mentally putting a face to the name. "He was a park ranger at Kenai Fjords National Park back when we worked together. He really liked you."

She snorted. "Teddy was an arrogant jerk. Who cares what he thought of me? I was engaged to you."

She was right. He shouldn't have cared that some other man, who'd clearly made no great impression on Poppy, had been interested in his fiancée. He turned his gaze back to watching the horizon and the boat slowed as he neared the inlet.

"You're frowning," Poppy said. "What's up?"

He shrugged. "It's nothing."

"You didn't let me get away with refusing to answer your question yesterday that I wanted to ignore," Poppy said. Her arms crossed over her chest.

"It probably sounds ridiculous now," Lex admitted, "but back when we were engaged Teddy overheard me saying that I wasn't sure I ever wanted kids. He pulled me aside and told me in no uncertain terms that if I wasn't able to give you what you needed, I should step aside and let you be with a man that would."

"Well, that's one the dumbest things I've ever heard," she said. "I'm a person not an object. I make my own choices about what I want and need, not some entitled weirdo at work."

She laughed but irritation flashed in her eyes,

"So, both Teddy and Johnny tried to talk you out of marrying me?" she asked. "Johnny because he thought I wasn't good enough for you, and Teddy who thought you didn't deserve me. I'd ask if there was anyone who didn't try to convince you that marrying me was a bad idea, but instead I'm more curious as to why you cared what anyone else thought as long as we were happy?"

He ran one hand over his face, wishing he had a good answer to that question, but realizing he didn't. She watched his face for one long moment, as if hoping for an answer. Then she turned away, giving up, and went back to join Stormy in the sheltered part of the boat.

Help me, Lord. He never had the courage to say the words he needed to say in the past. Turned out he still didn't now.

Finally, he saw the inlet ahead and slowly steered the boat into shore. He stopped the boat, dropped anchor and then leaped ashore and tied the rope to a huge and ancient tree jutting out of the rock for backup. When he turned to help Poppy, she and Stormy were already scrambling to shore. The dog began to sniff and within seconds she barked.

"Well, looks like we have the right place," Poppy said. She hitched her backpack up higher on her shoulder. Despite the waves of conflicting and confusing emotions that had passed between them on the boat, Poppy was all professional now as she and her K-9 partner traced their way along the shoreline. They found more candy wrappers, potato chip bags and general garbage that lay in between the crevasses, just like they'd found back at the cabin. Even without a word he could see her rancor at seeing how the poachers had littered, as well as her frustration over the fact that it was too muddy to be worth collecting for usable prints. A well-worn patch of mud and grass made it clear the path the poachers had used to climb up and down the glacier.

Stormy barked and indicated toward the slope.

"Go ahead," Poppy told her partner. "Just don't go far."

The dog licked her fingers as she reached to run her hand along the wolfhound's side. Then Stormy turned and galloped up the slope, her long legs moving far faster than either he or Poppy would ever be able to climb.

She glanced at Lex. "I'm going to head up there and join her."

"I'll be up in a second," Lex said. "I just want to take some pictures of the area. I do need to warn you, the glacier is huge. Just because the poachers used this as their entrance point doesn't mean the blue bears are still anywhere near this area."

"Got it." Her eyes lingered on his face for a split second, like she was about to say something more. Then she turned and made her way up the hill after Stormy, until finally she reached the top and he lost sight of her flaming red hair in between the dark green trees.

He let out a long breath and ran both hands over his face. His heart was so heavy from every aspect of the bear poaching case, and even though he knew that right now his small son was safe and being looked after, the lingering fear of the threat made against Danny still hung over him like a pending electrical storm.

And thinking of storms, he had absolutely no idea what to make of the charged moment between him and Poppy on the boat. It was unlike him to blurt out his own insecurities, no matter how incredibly true it had been.

It was also the first time he'd seen with his own eyes how much his getting caught up in other people's opinions of their relationship hurt her. He wasn't quite sure why he'd convinced himself so thoroughly that the fact she hadn't fallen apart when he'd called off the wedding meant she hadn't cared about him as much as he'd loved her.

Maybe he'd just been projecting his own insecurities onto her.

He glanced to the sky and prayed.

Lord, this might be the worst possible time for Poppy to be back in my life. But I'm also really glad she's the one here with me now. I can't imagine facing all this without her. Please, help me be the man You've called me to be, whatever Your plan.

"Lex!" Poppy's terrified voice cut through the air toward him, slightly strangled as if the last syllable of his name had caught in her throat, in a single word telling him everything he needed to know.

She was in danger.

"Hang on, Poppy!" he shouted. "I'm coming!"

He sprinted up the hill, even as his feet

slid underneath him on the slick ground, and he had to grasp on to rough brush and rocks for stability. Finally, he reached the top and ran into the thick trees, following a path so narrow it kept threatening to disappear with every step.

Then he saw Poppy standing stock-still, her right hand raised as if telling an unseen Stormy not to move.

A large brown bear towered before her, teeth bared, snarling and poised to strike.

EIGHT

Poppy froze face-to-face with the bear as it loomed over her, its mammoth claws just one swipe away from ending her life.

Years of training in how to handle a bear attack in the wild battled the overwhelming and palpable terror that had swept over her the instant she'd heard it roar. There was bear spray in the side pouch of her backpack. But from where she stood, there was no way to get it without flinching, and that could be deadly. As for the gun at her side, she wouldn't kill the bear unless it was absolutely necessary. Even then, considering how close it was to her, she might not even be able to get off a shot.

Brown bears were the deadliest of all the bears in Alaska.

There were two options to survive and she knew the guidelines better than anyone. Either be large—travel in groups, bang pots and make noise. Or in the worst-case scenario, become small, curl up into a ball and play dead. Neither were options now. She'd been foolish enough to walk through here alone.

Even worse, she'd put her partner in danger.

Poppy glimpsed past the snarling mass of teeth and claws roaring its intentions to end her, to where Stormy was tensed, crouched low and almost entirely hidden in the woods to her right. She'd had her eyes on the dog when the bear had reared in front of her, and hurriedly given her partner the signal to freeze. She knew the fearless wolfhound would attack the bear without hesitation. But she also knew that Stormy would probably be badly injured if she did.

Her partner might even be killed. Bears had been known to even charge at cars and other vehicles if they felt threatened. Her brave partner was just a pip-squeak in comparison. Poppy's heart beat so hard she could feel it pounding against her chest. She tried to pray, but her mind couldn't get further than, *Help me, God.*

"Poppy, don't move," Lex said from somewhere behind her. His voice was firm and strong, and seemed to cut through the fear welling up inside her. "Just stay calm and stay still. It's going to be okay."

How could he possibly know that? One wrong move on her part, and the bear would strike. And she couldn't save her own life without risking her partner's. She nodded as slightly as she dared, hoping Lex would see the motion and know she'd heard him. The bear growled a deep and guttural roar. Then Poppy heard Lex slowly and quietly walking into danger to stand beside her. Even without turning, she felt him lift the can of bear spray from her backpack. His arm brushed against her side and his fingers linked with hers.

"What are you doing?" she whispered.

"Strength in numbers," Lex said. "We look like a bigger, stronger force together."

The bear didn't move. Neither did Lex. He just stood there facing the bear, holding her hand and standing his ground.

"We have to protect Stormy," she whispered without even turning to look at him. "I don't want the bear getting her."

Her eyes fixed on her partner's shaggy face.

"I see her," Lex said softly. She heard the faint plastic and metallic clink of the safety cap being flicked off the can. "Now, I need you to take a deep breath, close your eyes and trust me. Okay?"

"Okay." She closed her eyes.

"Lord, help us."

In one swift motion, Lex pulled her into his chest with one hand and cradled her face against him. With the other, he detonated the spray. The bear roared in rage and pain. The thick vaguely acidic smell filled the air. She could feel Lex's heart beating against her chest and heard the sound of something crashing into the woods and felt Lex stepping back.

Then Stormy growled and Poppy opened her eyes to see the bear turn. It had finally realized Stormy was there. The disoriented bear charged on all fours toward Stormy. Snarling, the wolfhound leaped at the approaching animal, teeth bared. Partially blinded, the bear lashed out with a weakened blow that sent Stormy temporarily sprawling into the underbrush, only for Poppy's partner to leap up again, braced and ready for the fight.

The bear hesitated, the turned and lumbered off into the woods. Stormy barked furiously at the departing animal as if warning it not to return. Then she trotted over and butted her head against Poppy's hand. She wasn't even limping, let alone scratched or injured. The wolfhound's eyebrows raised as if asking if she should chase the bear. Poppy laughed. "Stay, Stormy. Good dog. You are such a very good dog."

Then she realized her other hand was still clutching Lex's.

She turned toward him and, as she did, her free hand grabbed ahold of his jacket collar.

"Thank you," she said. "Also, that was the single most reckless and dangerous thing you've ever done. Since when do park rangers run toward brown bears? This wasn't in any of the training I remember."

A cross between a laugh and a relieved sob choked in her throat as she said it. He chuckled softly and dropped the canister of bear spray. His other hand brushed the hair off her face.

"You're welcome," he murmured. "Now, are you okay?"

Suddenly it was as if the tension holding her limbs together gave way and her legs collapsed, almost sending her tumbling to the ground.

"Hey, it's okay, I've got you." He dropped her hand and wrapped both of his arms around the small of her back, pulling her into his chest. Then his right hand ran up the curve of her spine until it rested on her neck. "It's just the sudden jolt of adrenaline wearing off."

Poppy knew that, but it didn't change how good it felt to be held in Lex's arms. She reached her arms up and wrapped them around his neck.

"The bear will be fine, too," he added. "The spray will wear off in no time with no permanent damage."

"I know," she said. "You've never been the kind of person to kill an animal when there was a way you could save it."

"I would've to save your life," he said.

"I know." Just like she knew it might've been even more dangerous for him to fire a gun in a forest that dense where there was the possibility she or Stormy could be hurt. "But you'd be just as likely to wound it and then volunteer at an animal rescue to nurse it back to health."

He chuckled. "True, but hey, my plan worked, didn't it?"

"I said it was reckless," she said. "I never doubted it would work."

"I didn't know if you'd trust me."

"I've *always* trusted you," she told him.

Her face tilted up toward his and his arms tightened around her.

"And I will always be there when you need me," Lex vowed. "No matter where you go and no matter what happens in our lives, if you're ever in danger and you call on me, I will be there for you."

"I know," she admitted.

Before she could say anything more, his lips met hers. Lex kissed her and she kissed him back, both of them holding on to each other as if they'd never been apart.

Stormy growled with that soft rumble, warning her of danger. Poppy pulled back out of Lex's arms and turned to her partner, but not before she saw something like confusion fill Lex's eyes.

"What is it?" she asked her partner. "What do you sense? Show me."

Stormy barked and ran back the way they'd come. She followed, Lex beside her, until they reached the edge of the woods and looked down. A small nondescript speedboat had pulled up beside Lex's park ranger boat.

A thin masked figure in fatigues stood on the deck of their boat. The second larger one was untying it from the rock where Lex had fastened it.

The poachers were here, and they were stealing their boat.

Lex reached for his weapon, praying he wouldn't have to use it. Open cliffside lay before him, sloping down to the water below with no cover in sight. Both poachers were armed and once he stepped out of the trees he'd be an open target. But letting them steal his boat, leaving them stranded on a remote glacier, wasn't an option.

"Go," Poppy said. "I'll cover you."

Any doubt that she wouldn't never crossed his mind.

He took a deep breath, turned and ran down toward the water, knowing his best advantage was the element of surprise. Lex fired a warning shot in the air. It arched high above the larger man in camo who'd been trying to untie Lex's boat. The man yelped and leaped back.

But the thinner poacher wasn't as easily deterred. He turned from his post on Lex's boat and stepped up onto the side as if preparing to leap down. The poacher raised his weapon and aimed it directly at Lex as he scrambled down the cliff toward them. But he never got the chance to fire, as Poppy took aim. Her bullet rang off the side of the boat and ricocheted safely into the water, far enough away from the poacher so as not to risk hitting him, but close enough to startle him. The poacher slipped and fell off Lex's boat and into the cold Pacific waters. The larger man hesitated as if debating whether to return fire. But then Lex watched the man's face pale and in an instant he knew why, as Stormy leaped to Lex's side, charging down the slope beside him.

The thinner poacher scrambled from the water and back into his own boat, swearing and bellowing for his partner to follow. The larger poacher turned and ran after him, splashing knee-deep into the water and barely making it into the smaller boat as his partner gunned the engine. In seconds the small speedboat had disappeared from sight.

Lex paused on a narrow ledge and gasped a breath as he felt Poppy reach his side. They kept climbing down the slippery cliffside as quickly as they dared, letting Stormy take the lead.

"The precision of that shot," he said, "considering the distance was incredible."

"Thanks," she said. "I've had a lot of practice."

Lex imagined she had. But there was also a relaxed confidence that hadn't been there before. Back then she'd been so focused on the plans she'd made and guidelines she was following it was as if she believed that if she stuck to them precisely she'd be able to keep anything bad from happening to them. It had made her tense and on edge. He hadn't realized until long after he'd lost her how his impulsive way of canceling plans and dashing off to help his friends had made the situation worse and added to her stress.

Maybe he'd been a little harsh when he'd told her that they'd never been any good at being partners. After all, he hadn't exactly been focused back then on figuring out how to be the partner she needed.

As soon as they were all on board, the rope coiled and the anchor raised, Lex gunned the engine and they took off in the direction the poachers had gone. They searched the surrounding inlet, coves and islands for over an hour and came up empty. While the criminals didn't have too large a head start, there were just too many places a boat that size could hide in the sprawling national park, and the last thing Lex wanted was to be lured out of safe waters into a dangerous game of cat and mouse with a heavily armed foe.

Finally, they had no choice but to give up the hunt.

"The poachers won't return to that inlet," Poppy said. She leaned on the console beside him in the bow of the boat and looked out over the endless gray-blue water spreading out ahead of them. "They probably liked it because it was a secluded way to climb that glacier without too much risk of being noticed. Now that they know we've found that spot, the location is compromised. They'll regroup and find another route to get to the bears."

"I agree," Lex replied. "We can assume mother blue bear and cub won't be back to that inlet there, either, now that we know there's a territorial brown bear in that area. I'm just sorry we failed."

He sighed and ran his hand over the back of his head. Then, as his hand dropped back to his side, he felt Poppy take it and squeeze it hard.

"We didn't fail," she insisted. "If anything, we bought that little bear cub a bit more time and made it harder for the poachers to get her."

"I hope that you're right."

"I know in my heart that I am. And don't worry, Lex, we *will* find a way to stop them. Look, every time my team meets I'm sure we all have in the backs of our minds the knowledge that not every case we face is going to be solved immediately. Some are going to take weeks. Some might take months." She blew out a breath. "And yeah, I have no idea when we're going to find the missing bride or figure out what really happened up on that cliff. I don't know when we're going to help Eli find the Seavers for his godmother or Katie discover who's been poaching reindeer from her aunt's ranch. I just know it's going to happen. Just like I know we're going to stop these poachers."

Silence fell between them again and something caught in his throat that felt even deeper and stronger than the feeling that had surged through him when he'd impulsively held her in his arms and kissed her.

How was I ever blessed enough to have a woman like Poppy love me? How was I ever foolish enough to let her go?

He let the boat slow and just drift gently in the water, feeling like there was something he should say to the incredible woman standing beside him, but not even knowing where to start.

"I'm sorry I left you to arrange our future and plan our wedding on your own," he said. "You just seemed so good at organizing things. I just felt useless, like you didn't need my help. But for what it's worth, I'm sorry."

She blinked and for a long moment didn't reply.

"For the record," she said finally. "I never once doubted that if I was in crisis and really needed you that you'd be there for me. I knew, even after we'd gone our separate ways, that if I was in trouble I could call on you. You're really good at having people's backs."

Then she frowned.

"Is that a bad thing?" he asked.

"I didn't want to have to be in a crisis for you to be there for me," she admitted, a tinge of something almost like defiance filling her voice. "Yes, you were the kind of man who'd rush to help a friend in need. I liked that about you. I even loved that about you. But I needed the kind of man who'd also celebrate my success when I had an amazing day at work or who'd switch off his phone long enough to sit on the couch with me, watch a movie and eat pizza."

He smiled almost ruefully. "I seem to remember us eating a lot of pizza," he said.

But how many times had their dinners and date nights been interrupted by a friend calling his phone or even showing up at the door?

More than he liked to remember.

"I didn't want you to only be there when it counted or when you thought I couldn't handle it," she said. "I wanted all that everyday quality time that comes from sharing life with someone. Even if it meant boring meetings with people explaining how to get a mortgage or how many people could fit in a seating plan. I'm guessing Danny loves spending time with you. Not because he always feels useful or needed, but because he feels loved."

She paused and pulled her hand from his.

"I'm sorry, that's not the best analogy," she added. "After all, he's still a toddler. But maybe a better one is that I really, really love team meetings and hearing my colleagues brief their cases, even if I don't have all the answers or I don't end up doing anything more than sit there and cheer my teammates on while they solve the case."

"Both of those are good analogies in their own way," Lex murmured.

"You care about the same things I care

about," Poppy said, and something seemed to break in her voice. "You want to save people's lives, rescue animals and protect the natural world. All I wanted was for us to be a team. I didn't want you discussing your doubts with everyone else and avoiding all the tedious parts of being in a relationship. I loved you and wanted to spend the rest of my life with you, including the hard and boring parts."

His heart caught in his chest. Somehow hearing Poppy say that she'd loved him impacted him every bit as much as it had in the past, even if those feelings were gone. Water flowed beneath them and wind rushed past. Towering islands rose from the depths around the small boat.

"Maybe you were right and it was for the best you called off the wedding," she said quietly. "I don't want to be married to a man who's only there for me when my life's on fire."

"I didn't tell you I'd met your boss and gone to a trooper recruitment event because I felt embarrassed," Lex admitted. "When the woman you admired so much told me I wasn't cut out for the career you loved, I was afraid you'd think less of me. It took a long time for me to really process what I think she was trying to tell me."

"Which was?" Poppy asked, and he was thankful she hadn't questioned why he'd seemingly changed the subject.

"Your boss told me that I shouldn't apply to be a state trooper just because somebody else wanted me to," he said. "She said her hunch was that I tended to follow the lead of other people instead of making decisions for myself. It stung, but she was right. And to be fair, she also said a lot of great things about my skills and abilities, too, which helped."

The dock loomed ahead, and he steered the boat toward it.

"When Johnny first moved to Gustavus he stayed with us," Lex added. "I gave him a set of keys to the bed-and-breakfast, which was mostly symbolic because nobody ever really locks their doors here. When he moved out, I didn't ask for them back and let him know he could return if he ever needed to. Then, when he told me he'd heard about the blue bear poaching down at the watering hole, I asked for them back."

"That's more than fair," she said. "Especially if he was going to dodgy places or hanging out with potentially dangerous people."

"It's not like he was ever going to use them," Lex said. "It was just my way of taking a step and drawing a boundary, of deciding what I did and didn't want around Danny."

He blew out a hard breath.

"Bottom line is, I don't think I made a lot of deliberate choices like that back when we were together," Lex said. "I waited for you to ask for what you needed instead of trying to step up and figure it out for myself. I jumped up and ran whenever my friends called without pausing to even ask if there were other options, like drawing a line and telling them to call someone else, sleep it off, walk or call a cab. Your boss gave me a wakeup call, Poppy. I didn't fight for myself back then. I didn't fight for us."

Her lips parted like she was about to say something more. Then he heard her phone chime and watched as she pulled it out of her jacket pocket. She blinked as she read the message.

"Okay," she said, looking from the screen to his face. "That was Will. He says he's managed to interview what feels like half of Gustavus in the past few hours and has some unexpected news."

"Which is?"

"He'll explain when he sees us." She hesitated. "All I know is he says it looks like Johnny was lying to you."

NINE

They docked the boat and drove back to the house, small talk filling in the spaces between the silence and Lex's spinning mind. Fat and intermittent raindrops had started hitting the windshield again. Stormy was curled up in the back seat of his truck, and the woman who in less than two days had turned his life both inside out and upside down sat beside him on the passenger seat. Poppy's face was turned toward the window. His eyes traced the lines of the back of her neck.

Despite the fact she was sitting just inches away from him, he'd never missed her more.

When they reached the house, they found Will's truck in the driveway and the front door locked. A bit flustered, Lex searched his pocket a moment before coming up with the carabiner of mostly work keys that had his house keys on it, as well. He couldn't remember ever being locked out before and wondered if it had been his mom or Will that had done it.

They found Will in the living room sitting by the fire with Scout lounging at his feet, but they both jumped up when he and Poppy came in. Stormy made a becline for her water dish and Scout sauntered over to join her.

"Hope it's okay I locked the door," Will said, leaving Lex to wonder if he looked either confused or annoyed. "It's instinctual, and the back door was already locked."

"Probably a smart move," Lex told him. "We should keep the back sliding door locked, too. The windows all have safety latch locks to keep them from being opened more than a few inches. But before this, those were there to keep furry critters from sneaking in." He sighed. Had it really come to this? "Poppy said you've got news."

"I do," Will said. "I do need to brief our boss and told Lorenza I'd call as soon as you got back and Poppy was ready. But I wanted to give you a heads-up about something first."

"Okay." Lex braced himself for whatever the trooper was about to say. "Lay it on me. Poppy says you think Johnny was lying to me?"

"Absolutely everybody I spoke with today

agrees that Johnny Blair has not been to the watering hole, touched a drink of alcohol or hustled a game of pool or darts in over four months. So, that can't be where he found out about poaching blue bears."

Lex dropped into a chair, feeling like the wind had been knocked out of him.

"Are you serious?" he asked.

"Yup," Will said. "Trust me, it's hard to get that many different people to lie about the exact same thing without one of them cracking."

"Will is a really tough investigator," Poppy interjected. She sat down on the couch, opposite Lex. "He's naturally suspicious and doesn't fool easily. I'd trust his conclusion.'"

"Thanks," Will said. "I'm going to tell the team that, in my professional opinion, Johnny was telling the truth when he told you he hadn't been to the watering hole in months, and lying through his teeth when he told you that's where he heard about the blue bear cubs being poached." He shrugged his shoulders. "I don't know if that's good news or bad news from your standpoint, but that's what I think and that's what I'm telling the boss. There's more I'm going to brief the team on, but that's the main thing I wanted you to hear from me."

Lex wasn't sure how Poppy knew he needed a few moments to process the news. But she stood and walked over to the kitchen, where the two K-9s had been joined by the kitten and were now all chasing each other around the island, their paws slipping and sliding on the tiles like children on a frozen lake. She let the lot of them outside into the backyard, then went into her room and came out a few moments later in clean jeans and a T-shirt, with her lightly damp hair around her shoulders.

Will set his laptop up at the dining room table and started the video call. As before, Poppy and Will sat at the table in front of the screen, while Lex stood behind them. It was a much smaller group this time. Only Lorenza and Eli joined from the day's earlier meeting, along with a petite woman with shoulder-length auburn hair and a stylish gray business jacket who Poppy introduced as Lorenza's assistant, Katie Kapowski. All three of them shared one screen, with Lorenza in the center and the other two hovering on the edges.

"Nice to meet you," Lex said to Katie. "I've had the pleasure of meeting your aunt and I hope they find whoever has been stealing her reindeer."

Katie smiled. "Thank you."

They listened as Will gave a brief rundown of the results of his interviews in Gustavus today, along with the same conclusion he'd reached that Johnny had been lying through his teeth to Lex when he told him he'd overheard someone talking about the blue bear poachers.

"So, where else could Johnny have learned about the poaching?" Lorenza asked. She leaned back in her chair and crossed her arms. Her keen gaze seemed to fix on Lex's face.

"I don't know," he admitted. "As I mentioned before, we hadn't been close in a while. I do know he was dating Ripley and working at her brother's small tourism charter flight business."

"Well, whatever his source, he wanted to keep it from you," Will said. "Johnny has a record. Is it possible he was contacted by criminal elements from his past wanting his help? Maybe he turned them down and told you, and they killed him for it."

Sadness swelled inside Lex's core. "It's very possible."

"Is it also possible he was working with

them and double-crossed them after the first poacher was murdered or for other reasons?" Lorenza asked.

"I don't know," Lex admitted. "I hope not."

He felt Poppy reach her hand back subtly and squeeze his fingers for a moment before letting them go.

"What do we know about the charter airline?" Lorenza prodded.

"It's very small," Poppy said. "Two small planes, one that can carry two passengers and one that can carry four. It caters to tourists with money who want a private tour of the glaciers. Most are wealthy foreigners who fly into his small airport on their personal jets and then take a tour at a much lower altitude with Nolan in his prop plane. Then they leave again without ever coming into Gustavus. The only staff are Nolan, who runs it and flies, Ripley, who does admin, and Johnny, who did mechanical stuff and odd jobs. So, he could've overheard a client talk about poaching the bears and not wanted to risk losing his job."

Lex wasn't sure when Poppy had looked into Johnny's employer, but he wasn't surprised that she had. She'd always been thorough.

"Have you spoken to Nolan?" Lorenza asked.

"The airline was closed when I swung by there this afternoon," Will told her.

"And I just called Ripley from my room a few minutes before this meeting started," Poppy said. "She confirmed what I knew about the airline and told me it was closed today because they only opened when they had customers. She said she'd send me a list of recent clients tomorrow."

Lex thought about the large and thin figures in camo gear who'd tried to steal their boat and an odd thought crossed his mind. Johnny hadn't been covering for his girlfriend, had he? She and her brother couldn't be the poachers?

"Do you think she's lying about Johnny's death and how she got locked in the cupboard?" Lex mused.

"I think she genuinely loved Johnny and she's scared," Poppy said, "but there may well be more she either can't remember or is choosing not to tell us."

"Do they have an alibi for the boat attack today?" Eli asked, leaning into the frame.

"Only each other," Poppy replied. "Ripley says she and Nolan spent the entire day together."

"But neither Ripley nor her brother have

any form of criminal record," Will leaped in, as if anticipating Lorenza's next question. "Ripley's long-term ex-boyfriend, Kevin Wilson, is another story, though. He's been arrested multiple times for aggravated assault, and recently served eighteen months for assaulting Nolan and threatening Ripley. He got out of prison three weeks ago."

"Do we know where he is now?" Lorenza leaned forward.

"Not yet," Will said. "He skipped parole and disappeared."

Lex's mind flashed to the food wrappers in one of the cabins in the national park and his suspicion somebody had been squatting there.

"You're thinking something," Poppy said to Lex. She turned back and looked at him over her shoulder. "The image of you on the screen might be small, but I can still tell when wheels are turning."

"I'm thinking about the fact that before Johnny was murdered, before we discovered the poachers were after blue bears and knew somebody had started stalking my home, I thought we had a problem with squatters camping out in a cabin on the national park," Lex said. "It's possible Kevin came here, looking for Ripley, and was hiding out in the cabins. He could be involved with the poachers."

"We'll look into it," Will announced. "And if Kevin Wilson skipped parole, came to town and is working with the poacher to capture bear cubs, we will find him."

"Anything new online about the bear cub sale?" Poppy asked.

"Not yet." Eli shook his head. "It still lists the sale as taking place tomorrow. But I'm guessing they don't have the second bear cub, otherwise they'd be posting about it."

On that small shred of hope, the video call meeting ended.

Then conversations about poachers, killers and crime faded into the background as Gillian came home with little Danny, and somehow the house returned to the gentle domestic life of any other afternoon, even with the added guests. Lex played "town" with Danny outside in the backyard sandbox, building houses out of blocks and roads out of sand. Poppy sat by the window on her laptop and watched. After a while, Poppy came out with a small plastic jug of water and helped them add a lake and a river to their town.

Then Gillian called them in for dinner. Lex took Danny to wash the sand off him and made it back to the kitchen in time to help Poppy set the table. They sat down to eat, holding hands as they said grace, with Danny to Lex's one side and Poppy on the other. Conversation darted around the table as they chatted about fishing, hiking, baking and movies, like the topics were shared balloons they were all batting back and forth to keep from touching ground.

Finally, night fell, and he went upstairs and put Danny to bed. When he came back downstairs, he found Poppy, Stormy and the kitten curled up alone in the living room by the fire, just like they had been the night before when he'd come close to kissing her.

"Your mom says to tell you that she's gone to book club," Poppy said, looking up from her laptop. "And Will and Scout are heading to the watering hole, in case any of the locals feel more chatty at night."

So, they were there alone again in his living room, with the weight of the case, their past and the impulsive kiss they'd shared earlier hanging between them.

"Also, I wanted to say thank you for sharing your life with me today," she added. She closed her laptop and set it down on the couch beside her. "It's felt really nice chilling with you and your family this evening."

Yeah, he thought, it had been. More than nice, it felt natural. And it hurt in a way he couldn't put into words to know that in a day or two she'd be leaving again and going back to her life in Anchorage.

The thought of Poppy ever giving it all up to stay in Gustavus was unthinkable. And no one who genuinely cared for her would ever ask her to. Lex took a deep breath and looked down at where she sat, her hair loose around her shoulders and her features highlighted by the fire flickering in the low evening light. If only he knew how to begin to tell her just how much he regretted letting her go, despite all the incredible growth and blessings God had brought into his life during their time apart.

A low and deep rumbling came behind her, like the sound of a glacier about to break off and crash into the water. But it wasn't until Poppy leaped to her feet and turned to her partner that he realized where it was coming from.

Stormy was crouched to spring like she'd been before the bear, the gentle calm of the moment before all but forgotten. Her lips parted in a half snarl.

"Stormy!" Concern washed over Poppy's face. "What's wrong?" The dog woofed urgently. "Show me."

Stormy turned and ran across the living room and up the closest staircase to the second floor. Poppy and Lex pelted after her, one step behind the dog. Even before they reached the top of the stairs he heard a sound that sent terror pouring down his spine.

His little son was whimpering, a small plaintive and pitiful sound that Danny only made when he was too scared or hurt to scream.

Poppy froze as she reached the top of the stairs, laying her hand on Stormy's collar to make the dog pause, too, while they assessed the threat. He stopped one step behind her. An empty hallway lay ahead of them. Silence surrounded them, punctuated only by the faint sound of the K-9's lingering growl and his own son's tears. He prayed hard, beseeching God for Danny's safety and help in whatever lay ahead. Then, without a sound, Poppy stepped slowly down the empty hallway, Lex one pace behind her, toward his son's bedroom door.

They reached Danny's room. The door

flew open ahead of them, smashing against the wall with a deafening crash.

"Daddy!" The sound of Danny's whimpering grew to panicked sobs. "I... Want... Daddy!"

A lanky masked figure in camo fatigues stood in the doorway of Danny's bedroom, his sunken gray eyes as cold as a shark's as they fixed on Lex and Poppy.

In one arm he clenched Lex's son. With the opposite hand he held a gun.

"Don't move!" he said. "Or the kid dies."

The masked man blocked the doorway of Danny's small room. The barrel of the gun was pressed against the boy's side. Fear pooled in the child's eyes. She smelled rain in the air, but it wasn't until the poacher took a step back into the room that she noticed with a start that the window was open about four inches, caught on what looked like a safety lock. How had he possibly gotten in? She had no idea. All that mattered right now was that he was cornered, and he knew it. And he had little Danny in his grasp.

"What do you want?" Poppy asked. She stood in the hallway and faced the man down, keeping her motions just as slow and deliberate in the face of the criminal as she would a wild bear. Vicious killers were always the most dangerous when trapped. She could sense Lex standing stock-still by her left shoulder, his eyes on his son and whispered prayers for Danny's safety on his lips. Poppy's right hand tightened on Stormy's collar, signaling the animal not to move. Her other hand raised slowly to show the man that it was empty.

She willed her mind to block out everything but how she was about to protect the small child and save his life.

If only she had her weapon.

Help. Us. Lord.

"I want you to leave me alone to go about my business," the poacher snarled. He stepped backward, moving deeper into Danny's room. "Someone's been poking their noses around where they don't belong, trying to get in the way of me getting what's mine."

Did he mean Will's questioning? Her own online investigation? Something her team had dug into?

Whatever it was, she was pretty sure he wasn't lying.

"What do you mean?" she asked. She kept her voice low but firm. "What's yours? Do you mean the money you'll get for bear cubs you're trying to capture and sell? Those animals aren't yours."

"You don't get to tell me what's mine!" the poacher shouted. "So, here's what's going to happen. I'm going to take something that's yours and hold on to your kid as collateral to make sure the bear cub sale goes through with my client tomorrow without interference. Once the buyer has the bear cubs and I have my money, you'll get a call telling you where to pick him up. Turn around right now and walk away."

Fear beat through her heart. She could feel Stormy almost quivering with energy under her hand, coiled to leap into action to protect the little boy. Poppy stared the man down, her tactical mind calculating every piece of information she'd need to save Danny's life—from the man's build, to where he was standing in the room, to the position of the gun, to the way he was clutching Lex's son with one arm.

Her jaw set. "That's not going to happen."

"I'm leaving with this boy right now!" the poacher shouted. "You don't want to face the consequences of stopping me. So turn around and walk away. Now."

Poppy heard the floorboards creak slightly

behind her, as if Lex was shifting his stance. They were standing so close and yet she couldn't see his face or know what he wanted her to do. She just hoped he trusted her as much as she trusted him. The gunman shifted Danny around to the other side, as if struggling under just how unwieldy and heavy a squirming toddler was. *Come on, Poppy, think!* The poacher wasn't about to kill Danny here. He wanted the boy alive and unharmed for his collateral plan to work.

So, if he opened fire, it wouldn't be at Danny.

"Now, here's what's going to happen," the masked man said. "You're going to back up down the hallway. I'm going to walk out of here and you're not going to stop me."

"No." Her voice rose, calm and clear, with an authority that came from somewhere deeper than just herself, from her badge, her team and the legacy of her fellow officers. "Because I'm an Alaska state trooper, this is my K-9 partner and we're not about to let anything happen to Danny. So, set him down gently, drop your weapon and raise your hands now."

He snorted, pulled the gun away from Danny's side and pointed it right between Poppy's eyes. She heard the floorboards creak behind her and then she felt Lex's hand brush against her back for just a fleeting moment and yet filling her with strength. She swallowed her fear. As long as the only weapon in his hand was pointed at her, it wasn't pointed at Danny.

Poppy stroked the back of the dog's neck with her fingertips and felt the tension radiating through her fur. She knew everything inside Stormy wanted to leap into action to rescue Danny. It was her purpose. It was what she was trained for. Stormy wouldn't hesitate to risk her life for the child.

"I would've thought losing Johnny was enough incentive to show you we really meant business," the poacher said. "But apparently you wanted to learn the lesson the hard way."

Poppy let go of the K-9's collar. "Stormy! Attack!"

Snarling, Stormy leaped.

TEN

Stormy reared up on her hind legs and stretched herself to her full, ferocious seven-foot height. The man shouted a swear word in terror and swung toward the K-9. Danny slipped from his kidnapper's grasp, tumbling onto his bed. Poppy leaped for the toddler without hesitation, diving into the room, catching Danny up into her arms and cradling him to her chest. She turned back. Stormy had the poacher down on the floor of the bedroom, her huge paws on his shoulders. The assailant thrashed against the dog, his weapon still in his grasp, their struggle blocking her exit.

The gun fired.

Plaster rained down as the bullet struck the ceiling above their head. Poppy curled herself into a protective ball, shielding Danny with her body.

"I've got Danny!" she shouted. "He's safe!"

The poacher shouted in pain as Stormy's strong jaws clamped onto his arm. A second bullet ripped from the poacher's gun, shattering the window. Glass rained down around them. She and Danny were still caught in the middle, with no way to escape the room and just one stray bullet away from being seriously hurt.

"I can take him down!" Lex shouted.

"Okay," she yelled. "Stormy! Stand down!"

She looked back, cradling Danny's small head into the crook of her neck. Lex's strong shoulders filled the doorway, blocking the kidnapper's path. Stormy sprung back. The perp stumbled to his feet, then as she watched, he turned and threw himself through the broken glass of the second-story window, shoulder first, like a desperate football player trying to block a tackle. He crashed through and into the rain outside.

"Keep my son safe!" Lex shouted.

"I will!" she called. "I promise!"

Without hesitation, Lex ran toward the shattered window and dove through. She looked out. The poacher scrambled and slid across the slippery roof of the covered porch below them. Lex tackled him. The two men struggled for a moment, rolling and battling in the darkness. Then the roof gave way under their weight and they fell through, landing on the lawn in a mass of limbs and broken boards.

The perp recovered first, leaping to his feet and sprinting across the lawn into the blackness of the night beyond. In an instant, Lex was on his feet and running after him. She lost sight of them in the darkness.

Stormy whimpered softly as if asking permission to jump through the second-story window and charge after them.

"Stay," Poppy said, unexpected tears choking her voice. "Good dog."

A moment later she heard an engine roar to life and then a few seconds later a second vehicle, which she recognized as Lex's. So, the poacher was trying to get away and Lex was chasing him. She prayed for his capture.

She ran her hand down Danny's back and gently tousled his hair, thankful he'd stopped crying. Okay, his breathing was strong, there were no obvious bruises or contusions and how hearty his cries were earlier were very good signs. *Thank You, God.* She'd give him a more thorough checkout in a moment, but first she had to get him away from the mess and chaos of the room.

The little boy's tearstained face looked up into hers and suddenly it hit her—Lex had entrusted her with the most important thing in the entire world to him, without even a moment's hesitation.

"Everything's going to be okay," she soothed, looking into Danny's wide and trusting eyes. "You're safe."

She stood slowly, holding him gently and asking God's help to keep the promise she just made to the little boy. She slid her phone out of her pocket and texted Will what had happened and that she was now with the toddler. Will texted her back an instant later that he would inform the team, contact Gillian, try to reach Lex and would head back to join her ASAP. She breathed a sigh of relief, knowing Will had it covered and all she now had to worry about was Danny.

Truly, the most important job of all.

She kept praying while she scooped up all the stuffed animals on the bed, along with Danny's blanket, and cradled them around him like a nest. Then she carried him out of the bedroom, with Stormy by her side, leaving the tossed mess of the room with shards of glass and plaster covering the floor behind. She closed the bedroom door behind her firmly and then looked down at Stormy. The dog peered up at her solemnly under shaggy brows as if Stormy felt the responsibility, too.

She started down the stairs with Danny in her arms and her K-9 partner by her side. A tiny hand brushed her face.

"Daddy." Danny sniffled. "Want Daddy!"

"I know, I wish your Daddy was here, too," she admitted, "but you and I, and Stormy, are going to go hang out in my room until he gets back."

"And Mu'shoom kitten?" Danny asked hopefully.

If she could figure out where the kitten was hiding, considering she'd probably been frightened by the chaos. "Yes, and Mushroom the kitten, too."

She checked that the front, back and sliding door to the kitchen were all locked, then went into her bedroom suite. She'd barely managed to lock the door when she'd heard a small but persistent scratching sound and opened it to see the kitten shoot past and dive under the bed. Stormy positioned herself against the door, with her head on her paws and her ears perked. *All right, then, the gang's all here.* Poppy locked the door again, climbed up on the bed with Danny and curled up beside him.

"Now," she said, keeping her voice playful and light, "we're going to play a special wiggling game. I'm going to point to different parts of your body and you're going to show me how good you can wriggle it, okay?"

Danny nodded enthusiastically. She breathed a sigh of relief, then sat cross-legged on the bed and methodically started checking the boy for any external or internal injuries. First, she started by having him follow her waving finger with his eyes, to help rule out the possibility of a concussion. Then had him wiggle his feet, kick his legs, waggle his fingers and wave his arms, while he laughed and giggled at the game. She laughed along with him, feeling tears of relief brush her own cheeks. His color and breathing were good, his pulse was strong, he had no bruises or scrapes and nothing was broken.

When she'd run through everything in her mental emergency first-aid checklist, she hugged him tightly and felt the little boy hug her back.

Thank You, God. Just thank You so much.

A gentle knock sounded on the door and Stormy's ears twitched slightly but her body didn't tense. Her heart leaped, hoping it was

Lex, but instead Poppy heard Will's voice. "How's it going?"

"Good." She looked down at the little boy in her arms. "Is Lex back?"

"Not yet," Will said. "It's just us for now. Scout and I are going to do a perimeter search and make sure all the exits and entrances are secured."

"See if you can find out how he got in," she told him. "I checked the doors, too. The window was only open a few inches and the porch roof didn't look strong enough to climb up."

"Will do," he said. "You're going to hold tight there?"

She swallowed hard. There were a dozen very important things related specifically to her training as a trooper she could be doing right now, and yet as she felt the small boy nuzzle against her she knew there was nowhere else she'd rather be. "I will."

Danny's small hand brushed the side of her face. "Read story?"

"Yes." Poppy looked down into his big eyes. "That sounds like a wonderful idea." She turned back to the door. "Will? Can you pop up to Danny's room and grab us some of his storybooks?"

Will came back with the books in moments. Poppy thanked him and locked the door behind him. She checked her phone in vain for texts from Lex, and seeing none, she set her phone down and turned to Danny.

"Okay," she said brightly. "Which one should we read first?"

He grinned. "Pi'gon story!"

Stormy gave up her post at the door and climbed across the bottom of the bed as Poppy tucked her legs up to make room for her. Mushroom slipped out from under the bed, balled up beside Stormy and started purring. Then, finally, Danny curled himself into the crook of Poppy's arm. She leaned forward and brushed a kiss on the top of his head, and she started to read.

She had no idea it was possible for a heart to feel both so light and so heavy at the same time. Was it possible to mourn the marriage and family she never had, while still being thankful for the amazing lives she and Lex had without each other? Could gratitude and grief, joy and pain, coexist inside her heart?

She settled back against the blanket, feeling Danny rise and fall on her chest with each breath. Maybe on some level she'd blamed herself for losing Lex. After all, if she'd been a better partner and done a better job of loving him, he would have stayed, right? And yet, at the same time, if he'd blamed himself for Johnny's life going down the wrong path she'd be the first to point out that no matter how hard and genuinely a person loved someone, they weren't responsible for that other person's choices.

And with those conflicting thoughts swirling inside her, she let her mind both leave the sadness of the past and the anxiety of the future, and exist in the present moment of the stories on the page, the animals snoring by her feet and the precious child in her arms.

A torrent of rain beat down around Lex's truck, streaming down the windows and clattering on the roof as if trying in vain to drown out his thoughts. He'd been chasing taillights on narrow, rural roads through the dark Alaskan wilderness for almost half an hour, and was no closer to catching the masked gunman. His gas light had been on for at least half of that, warning him that his tank was almost empty, and his windshield wipers were working overtime as they beat furiously against the rain.

The twin lights ahead disappeared as the

poacher cut onto a rough road through the trees, then reappeared ahead of Lex as he made the sharp turn after them. It had been like that since they'd left the outskirts of Gustavus—the lights seeming to blink off and then on again, as the truck swerved and weaved, then growing smaller as the truck sped away, then larger as Lex caught up.

He had to catch him. This man had threatened the life of his child, taken the life of his friend and was endangering the lives of rare bear cubs. And yet, after throwing everything he had into the chase, Lex was no closer to catching him.

Lex could feel the steady drag of his truck beneath him, letting him know it was pretty much down to running on fumes. The headlights ahead disappeared in the darkness and this time they didn't return, no matter how fast he drove or how intently he peered through the storm looking for the poacher. Had he taken a turn Lex had missed? Had he recklessly turned off his lights and either kept driving without them or hidden somewhere?

He had no idea. All he knew was that his truck was minutes away from running out of gas and the man he was chasing was gone. But even then, he kept driving, watching minute after minute tick by, until finally he admitted defeat and pulled over to the side of the road.

Lex leaned his head against the steering wheel. Hot tears pressed unshed behind his eyes.

"Help me, Lord, I feel like such a failure," he prayed out loud. "I don't even know who this guy is, how to stop him or what I'm supposed to be doing right now."

Truth was, he felt like he'd never been enough or done enough. As a kid, he'd done his very best to please his father, but that hadn't stopped his dad from losing his temper all the time and then eventually walking out on them, never to be heard from again. Lex had gone all out to help friends like Johnny change their lives, and yet they'd still made terrible decisions. He'd cared about two women and both relationships had failed—the first because he'd felt inferior and bailed on their wedding, and the other because she'd left him. He loved his son with his entire being and yet he hadn't been able to catch the man who'd tried to kidnap him.

"Is all this my fault, God?" he asked. "Did I do something wrong? Because it feels like

I've let everybody down and I don't know what You want me to do to fix it."

A song he'd heard once at a summer camp as a kid buzzed through his brain, around and around like a fly, telling him that if he did what was right everything would always work out for him. For the first time in his life, he found himself questioning just how overly simplified that message he'd internalized was.

As he stepped out of the truck into the pouring rain, bowed his head and walked around to the back of his truck, he found something Jesus said in the gospels cross his mind—God sends rain on both the just and the unjust. A grin crossed his face. *Yeah, wasn't that the truth?* He'd lived long enough already to see bad things happen to amazing people, like his mother, and great things happen to people who did terrible things. And, if he was honest, he'd also had some blessings in his life beyond what he ever hoped and deserved.

After all, he knew that Poppy was keeping his son safe right now.

He reached the back of his truck, opened the tailgate and thanked God his emergency gas canister felt heavy when he picked it up and sloshed it. A moment later he found his funnel, too. Other things that Jesus had said crossed his mind as he pulled off the gas cap and poured fresh fuel in the tank. There'd been a story about a man born blind, and while others had been worrying about whose fault the blindness was, Jesus had brushed all that talk away and focused on actually helping the guy.

Maybe that was what he should be focusing on right now, too.

It was a long drive back, prayers and doubts mingling inside him like the raindrops merging into streams on his windshield.

When he got back to the bed-and-breakfast, the front door was locked, but before he could even fish his keys out his mom opened the door. He stepped in out of the downpour. Wordlessly Gillian hugged him.

"He got away, Mom," he said hoarsely. "I tried my best, but I lost him."

"You'll get him next time," his mom reassured him.

And he almost laughed. Yeah, she said that about most things.

They walked into the living room and he was surprised to find it empty. "Where is everyone?"

"Danny's asleep," she said. "Will's upstairs

in Danny's room, nailing down a piece of plywood over the broken window and helping me move Danny's bed into my room." She gave her son a hard look as if guessing what he was thinking. "And don't say he should sleep in your room instead, because we both know you won't be sleeping tonight."

Yeah, that was true enough.

"What about the port of entry for the break-in?" he asked.

"Apparently, there was no break-in," she said. "According to Will, looks like whoever tried to kidnap Danny used a house key, unlocked the back door and walked in. He found fresh scratches on the keyhole like someone was trying to unlock it in the dark and a bit of mud tracked in the back door." Gillian shook her head and frowned. "And before you ask, I double-checked my keys right away. They're still in a zip pouch in my purse and haven't been touched."

What could that possibly mean? There were only three sets of keys to the house—his mom's, his and the one he once gave Johnny. But he'd demanded Johnny's keys back when his buddy told him about the blue bears being poached and said he'd been drinking again. Lex reached into his pocket and pulled out his key ring. Sure enough, both sets of keys were still there—his and Johnny's.

Had someone copied a set of their keys? If so, who and when?

"We need to get the locks changed," he said.

"Agreed," Gillian concurred. "I've already been calling around and found someone from the church who can do that for us first thing tomorrow."

"Thank you." He blew out a long breath. "Where's Poppy?"

"With Danny," his mom said. Her lips twisted like she was debating whether or not to say something more. Instead, she waved at Lex to follow her and started down the hallway. She reached the door of Poppy's suite, pressed a finger to her lips to signal for quiet and then eased the door open a crack. He peeked in.

There was Poppy curled up asleep with Danny tucked safely in the crook of her arm, with the toddler's head on her shoulder and her flaming red hair fanned out around them. Lex pressed his hand against his heart, feeling something tighten in his chest. Stormy was stretched out across the end of the bed by their feet with the kitten snuggling against her snout. The wolfhound's eyes opened and silently she looked at him.

"Good dog, Stormy," he whispered, and his voice caught in his throat. "Thank you for protecting my son."

He eased the door closed again. As he turned back, he found his mother's eyes on her face.

"I won't ask if you still have feelings for her," Gillian whispered as they walked away from the door, "because anyone with eyes in their head can see that you do. I'm not even going to ask if you think she'd be a good mother to Danny, because I know she would be. She's a good person who loves hard, works hard and can do anything she puts her mind to."

Her shoulders rose and fell, and he was suddenly reminded just how much his mother had always genuinely liked Poppy.

"But?" he asked softly.

"But as I told you back when you guys were planning on getting married, I don't like the way you used to get around her," Gillian admitted. "It was like you doubted yourself, shrunk and got smaller. She made you feel inferior."

He shook his head. Yeah, he remembered

his mom saying this just before he'd ended things with Poppy and called off their engagement. Although he'd never told Poppy, that conversation had been the one he'd accidentally left on her voice mail and the person he'd been admitting his doubts to was his mother.

"That doesn't make sense," Lex admitted, "because having Poppy by my side made me feel like a better and stronger man than I ever felt without her."

"I know," Gillian said. "But it was like she was a balloon and you thought you were only flying because you were holding on to her string, and since you lost her you've started to grow your own wings. I'd hate to see you lose yourself again now."

He heard a click and turned as the door to Poppy's suite eased open behind them. There she stood, in her stocking feet, with her hair slightly disheveled, a sleeping Danny in her arms and the most beautiful smile he'd ever seen in his life on her face. She looked so happy and so relaxed he was pretty sure she hadn't caught the contents of their conversation.

"Hey." Poppy smiled as she looked from Lex to Gillian and back. Then worry filled her eyes as they searched Lex's face. "He got away?"

He felt himself nod, but it was his mother who spoke first.

"Here," Gillian said, reaching out her hands for Danny. "Let me take him upstairs. I've got his bed made up in my room." She eased the sleeping boy into her arms. "I'll leave you two to talk."

His mother headed upstairs. The bedroom door swung open wider as Stormy pushed her way through. Mushroom darted past and disappeared down the hallway, leaping over the dog's feet. Stormy rubbed her head against Poppy's side. Then the K-9 butted her head against Lex, as well, as if to say hello, then wandered down the hall, leaving just Lex and Poppy.

"I'm sorry I lost him," Lex started. "He got a head start and was a pretty reckless driver."

"Don't worry about it," Poppy said. She ran both hands through her hair. "Happens to the best of us. We'll find him again."

And there was something about the way she said it that was so strong and determined he believed her.

"Thank you for taking care of Danny," he murmured.

"I loved spending time with him."

She started to walk past him, down the hallway and back to the living room. But as she passed, his hand reached out and touched her arm. She stopped and turned back.

"I'm sorry if this is speaking out of turn," Lex said, "but when you stopped outside Danny's door last night and didn't come during story time, I wondered if you were avoiding him or felt uncomfortable around him."

"You were right," Poppy admitted. "But only because I felt weak and didn't want it to impact you, or Danny, or this case."

He blinked. Of all the many words that filled his mind when he thought of Poppy, *weak* had never been one of them. He opened his mouth, but couldn't find anything to say.

"I told you," she said, "when you left it tore me open inside. I might not have cried in front of you, sent you a bunch of angry messages or vented about it on social media. But it hurt me so much I haven't been close to anyone like that ever since because I was afraid of being hurt like that again. And I guess I was afraid getting close to your son would make that old wound open up again." Then she smiled. "But I'm glad I got to bond with Danny, because he's absolutely amazing. Thank you for sharing him with me. I'm so happy for you and the life you've built here."

"Poppy…" His hand took hers. "I'm sorry I wasn't stronger back then."

"I'm sorry I wasn't braver," she said softly. "But when I think about Danny, and Stormy, and my team, and the lives we have now, I'm really happy for who we became."

"Me, too," he confided. "I only wish I didn't have to lose you for us to find it."

She squeezed his fingers and he squeezed hers back. They stepped closer together in the darkened hallway until the only thing between them was their joined hands.

The sound of a ringing phone filled the narrow space. But it wasn't until Poppy leaped back and snapped her cell to her ear that he realized it was hers.

"Hello?" she said. "Hey, why are you calling so late?… Oh." Her face paled as she met Lex's eyes. "Okay, we'll be right there. Bye."

She hung up the phone and sighed.

"That was Eli," she told him. "He says, bad news is we're too late and the poachers already have the second bear cub. Good news is they think they've figured out where the poachers are taking the cubs. But we have to act now. Otherwise we'll lose any hope of rescuing the cubs forever."

ELEVEN

"So, turns out some people are more chatty around the watering hole at night," Will said as the three of them stood around the table in the darkened living room and waited for the video call to start. "Not that I know if any of the gossip I turned up helps us in solving the case. But it might give you some insight into what your friend Johnny was going through, Lex, at the very least."

"Thanks," he said, "I appreciate it."

The long drive in the rain, praying after losing sight of the poacher, had helped get his heart and mind right. While there were still a lot of answers Lex didn't have and things he had to figure out—especially in terms of dealing with whatever those invisible threads were that kept tugging him back toward Poppy—he definitely had more peace in his heart about Johnny, and for that he was thankful.

"Go on," he added. "Lay it on me."

"All right," Will said. "Remember I'm dealing in small-town gossip here, not fact. But rumor has it that Ripley's ex-boyfriend, Kevin Wilson, made a beeline here to find her after he got out of jail. Nolan has been complaining to anyone who'd listen that Kevin's been coming by both the house and the airplane charter business, trying to get Ripley back and making trouble. The way Nolan apparently tells it, he chased him off and told him not to come back."

"You sound skeptical of that," Poppy remarked.

"I'm always wary of anyone who paints themselves as the heroic good guy of the story," Will said with a shrug. "But Kevin does have a record for assault, not Nolan."

"Any idea why Kevin went to jail for an assault charge?" Lex asked. "Had to have been pretty major if it wasn't dealt with by probation."

"I can answer that one!" Eli's voice broke through and they glanced to see the tech's face on the screen. "Kevin Wilson has multiple charges for assault and issuing threats, against both Ripley and Nolan. The incident that put him in jail apparently involved smashing Nolan's truck with a baseball bat."

Will whistled under his breath.

"All because he wanted Ripley back?" Poppy asked.

"Looks like it," Eli said. "But looks can be deceiving. Kevin also tried to sue both Nolan and Ripley for lawyer's fees, pressing false charges and lost wages, and it was thrown out."

"That tracks," Will said. "Rumor is Kevin came around the watering hole looking for Ripley and Nolan a week ago, claiming they owed him money for sending him to jail. Maybe Johnny's boobytrapped his house to keep him from breaking in."

Lex looked from Will to Eli on the screen, and then finally at Poppy.

"Then why aren't you hauling this Kevin guy in for questioning?" he asked.

"He alibied out," Will said. "Kevin left town a few hours before Johnny died. Nolan flew him to Juneau personally just to get him out of town. Nolan showed me the flight record proving he was in the air with Kevin when Ripley and Johnny were attacked at the house. From there Kevin hopped on a flight to Anchorage. Nolan's also got both text and phone records showing Kevin's phone calling Nolan and Ripley from Anchorage."

"So, Nolan and Ripley have every reason to hate Kevin and yet they're also his alibi," Poppy said.

"And vice versa," Will noted.

Lex let out a long breath and ran his hand over his head.

"So, we've got nothing," Lex muttered.

Except, as Will said, a window into what Johnny was dealing with. Lex couldn't imagine Johnny dealt well with his girlfriend being harassed by her ex. Johnny was nothing if not loyal and protective.

"Good news is that I finally got the recent client list from Ripley and Nolan," Will added. "Took some persuading as his clients are mostly rich, foreign tourists who like privacy. But we've got people on here from all over Europe, the Persian Gulf and Asia. Any one of which might have been scheming with the poachers to capture the baby bears and then killed Johnny when he caught wind of it."

"Which is a fantastic transition to why I called you for a late-night chat," Eli said, drawing their attention back to the screen.

"The whole team will be meeting tomorrow morning and Lorenza is off tonight at a charity event as we speak. But I thought you would want to know now, so she gave me the go-ahead to brief you. I'm sending a package of files through for you to print, so you've got a copy of everything I'm looking at. Long story short, I found a post on the dark web saying both bears will be going up for bid at an illegal animal auction in less than forty-eight hours. They've also apparently got a two-or three-year-old brown bear."

Poppy blew out a hard breath. Nobody in their right mind would try to poach a fully grown bear, no matter how greedy or desperate they were for money. "That doesn't give us a lot of time."

"Less than you'd think," Eli said. "Because also according to dark web chatter the bears are due to be smuggled out of Glacier Bay by boat, to meet up with a ship near Anchorage just before dawn and then from there head out into international waters. We don't know where they'll be headed yet, could be Asia but probably Russia. So, obviously we'll be coordinating with the coast guard on this. Once they've left American waters everything gets a lot more complicated."

And if that happened, Lex knew animal trafficking well enough to know that would probably mean the bears would be gone for good.

Will looked at Poppy. "Guessing that means we'll be heading to Anchorage and coordinating with the coast guard."

"That's not for me to say," Eli said. "But I know the boss wants to talk to you first thing in the morning."

Lex felt Poppy's gaze on his face but didn't dare let himself look her way in case his eyes gave away how he was feeling. The lightness he had felt in his heart earlier now seemed to sink inside him like a stone. So, one way or another, it sounded like Poppy was leaving his life tomorrow.

He didn't notice when Will pushed the button on the laptop to send things through wirelessly to print, but was thankful when he heard the printer in his office spring to life, because it gave him a reason to turn his back on the conversation and head to the other side of the room. Lex took the sheets Eli had sent off the printer and looked down at the crude posts, with pictures of the sad bear cubs and a description of the terrible fate that awaited them. But somehow his eyes found it hard to focus.

He'd never expected Poppy to suddenly land in his life, let alone thought that she would stay. So why did the thought of her leaving weigh so heavily inside him?

"This doesn't sit right with me," Poppy said, her voice drawing his attention back to the conversation happening around the table. She reached out for the papers in Lex's hands, took them from him and then spread them out. "A poacher goes after Lex's son, tries to kidnap him and says he's taking the kid for collateral until he can sell the bears to his client tomorrow."

"You mean, until the bears are safely on the boat and heading out into international waters," Will clarified.

"No." Poppy shook her head. "That might be what he meant but that's not remotely what he said. He said he was taking Danny until he got his hands on the second bear cub, which he apparently didn't have yet, and sold them both to his buyer." Her emerald eyes met Lex. "Right? Can you back me up on this?"

"I can," Lex said. He grabbed a kitchen chair and sat down beside her, until he was eye level with Will and could see the screen.

"My mind was most definitely a mess at the time, but I'm pretty sure she's right about the second cub thing. And I distinctly remember him saying he had a buyer."

"A buyer," Will repeated. "Singular?"

"Yup," Poppy confirmed. "One he was meeting tomorrow."

"Well." Will leaned back in his chair. "That sounds a bit different than an overseas animal auction."

Eli raised his hands, palms up.

"Hey, don't shoot the messenger," he said. "I'm just reporting what the internet is saying. Not that I've verified it's true."

"We know," Poppy told him.

She ran her finger over her lip in a subtle gesture that Lex knew meant she was thinking.

"People do lie," he said after a long moment. "He was kidnapping my son, after all."

"People lie for a reason," Poppy countered. "They do it to get out of trouble or to get some advantage. Why not just tell us he's kidnapping Danny until the boat leaves? Why lie and say he doesn't have the second bear cub yet or that he already has a buyer?"

Lex looked from Will to Eli, waiting for

one of them to answer. Instead, Poppy's gaze was fixed on him.

"I don't know," he said, feeling flustered. "Maybe because they still hadn't captured the second bear cub by that point and coming after Danny would keep us from stopping them or act as a distraction."

"But *why*?" she prodded. "Why not just go capture the bear cub? Why come here first?"

"Maybe he tried to grab Danny and when that didn't work he went and captured the bear cub?" Lex suggested. "No, that doesn't make sense. Because he wasn't out of my sight long enough to travel into the park, get to the glaciers, capture a bear, come back and post it online. So, I don't know, maybe he has an accomplice or there's more than one set of poachers? But again, that doesn't make complete sense."

He looked down at the printouts spread on the table. There were some new pictures of the bears, one in a cave and a couple side by side in cages. He frowned. It was like his subconscious was telling him there was something wrong with the pictures but he couldn't place it.

"Either the kidnapper lied, something in

the post is false or these were done by two separate people," he added.

He glanced at Poppy's face and suddenly realized the smile that had ignited in her eyes had that same spark as when they used to jog together, urging each other on, making one another faster and stronger.

"Thank you," she said. "My brain gets too caught up on one way of thinking sometimes and hearing you come up with different ideas always helps with that." She looked back at Will and Eli. "Lex is right. Something doesn't mesh here."

Lex glanced back down at the papers in front of them and blinked as he finally realized what he was seeing. No, it couldn't be.

"*Wait.* These two bear cubs are the same bear!" he exclaimed, pointing from one to the other. "They just switched it from one cage to another and took it from a different angle to look like it's two different animals."

Poppy met his eyes and finished his thought. "But they still only have one bear."

Eli shook his head. "Why didn't I see it?"

"Because you're a tech guru, not an animal expert," Poppy said. "I'm sure if they'd added a weird filter you'd have caught it immediately. Was this posted after I reported the attempted kidnapping attempt?"

"Yup," Eli confirmed.

"Then it's still possible we can stop the second bear cub from being poached," she said. "No second bear cub means no boat leaving first thing tomorrow for the animal auction, means more time to find and stop them. Of course, it's always possible they already have a buyer lined up and the auction is a ruse, too." She turned to Lex. "How do we find the second bear cub before they do? Any guesses?"

All eyes turned to him. Right, so everyone was counting on him to figure out the location of a rare baby bear cub in one of the world's largest national parks based on a few pictures where he knew the bears had been, and his own intuition.

He prayed for wisdom. Then he felt Poppy's hand take his and squeeze it.

"You've got this," she said. "And don't worry about getting it wrong. My whole theory about this case might be, as well, and we all get it wrong on this team sometimes."

Had she always been so understanding and he'd been too caught up in his own insecurities to see it? Or had she mellowed with time and teamwork? Maybe it didn't matter—they were here now. *Lord, help me see what I need to see.* His eyes scanned the new posts, the printouts from the day before and a map of Glacier Bay. Then he took a deep breath.

"Okay, this is just an educated guess" he began. "But judging by the shading in this background of this picture here, this cub is near an ice cave." He pointed out each step of his explanation as he went. "Due to the time of year, the location of the bay we found where the poachers were coming ashore and the usual roaming habits of bears, I'm thinking that if the second cub wasn't poached she's likely with the mama bear somewhere near…here."

His finger came to stop on a small inlet about twenty minutes away by boat from where they'd stopped earlier.

"So, Lex and I head there," Poppy said without a moment's hesitation. "We look around and see what we can find."

"Sounds good." Will nodded. "Scout and I will stay here and cover the home front and make sure Gillian and Danny are safe."

"Perfect," Poppy continued. "Worst-case scenario and there's nothing there, everyone will still go ahead with the existing mission as planned to locate, investigate and intercept any potential ship taking the bears overseas for an illegal animal auction. We're just making sure we're covering our bases."

"Hey, I'm not saying we'll find anything," Lex added quickly. "It's just a guess."

"An educated guess, based on your experience, knowledge and expertise," Poppy reminded him. She reached over and squeezed his hand again, this time not letting go as quickly, and as her eyes met his for a split second it felt like they were the only two people in the room. "Whatever we find, I believe in your hunches and think it's worth pursuing."

"Looks like Lorenza's evening plans are being interrupted, after all," Eli chimed in.

"But knowing her, she won't mind a bit," Will said with a chuckle. "But whether the poachers have got a buyer already lined up to buy the bears tomorrow or they're shipping out by boat to an overseas auction in the morning, it sounds like this case is wrapping up within a few hours one way or the other."

Lex took a deep breath as an unexpected pain filled his chest.

In other words, one way or the other, Poppy was leaving his life and going back to Anchorage tomorrow.

* * *

As expected, Lorenza wasn't the slightest bit bothered when Poppy called and interrupted her evening and was quick to sign off on their plan to check out the location Lex had identified on the map. It felt good to have her boss believe in her, even when she was chasing a hunch. In fact, Lorenza seemed even more concerned at how tight the timeline was and suggested expanding the mission into a stakeout. Poppy, Lex and Stormy would make their way to the glaciers, locate the area Lex had suggested and hunker down for a few hours somewhere to see if there was any suspicious activity. Then, if there was nothing by sunrise, they'd come back to Gustavus and regroup with a video meeting with the rest of the team.

Poppy napped for a few hours, ate a late dinner and packed some snacks, then got dressed into her rugged outdoor gear and met Lex outside by the truck shortly after 2:30 a.m.

It was a quiet drive through the Alaskan wilderness at night to the national park, punctuated only by the sound of the engine purring, the tires brushing the road beneath them and Stormy's softly wheezing half snores coming from the back seat.

At first Poppy didn't think much of the fact that she and Lex had barely exchanged two words since leaving, and for that matter not really talked much after ending the video call with Eli. After all, she was exhausted and she imagined he was, too, if not more so. Her body ached from being up and moving in the middle of the night on too little sleep, along with the wear and tear of having fought for her life more than once in the past couple days. She felt like she needed to sleep for a week, or at least a solid twelve hours, to rest and recuperate.

Considering the physical strain of what Lex had gone through, she was sure his body was pretty sore, too.

She glanced his way. The darkness of the night around them had deepened his eyes and cast long shadows down the line of his jaw. Lex seemed older than he had in her memories, but more handsome and wiser, too, like his heart and mind had been weathered by the life he'd lived without her.

She turned and looked back out the window, knowing they only had a few hours left in each other's lives and yet not knowing what to say. The sky had cleared, leaving a tapestry of bright stars shining above them.

No, there was more to the weariness inside her than just what her body had gone through. Her heart felt tired and heavy, too, like she'd put all of her painful and complicated feelings for him on ice when he'd broken her heart, but in the past two days they'd all come back demanding to be felt. She had no idea what to say to the amazing, complicated and incredible man sitting beside her and no clue where to even start, so she sat and prayed, and even let her mind drift a little as they drove to the national park.

"I'm fairly confident that we weren't followed," Lex said as they reached the docks. "I took a route that's near impossible to drive without headlights on and tight enough in places that I should've seen running lights."

They got out of the truck and walked down to where the water lay a deep and black roll of velvet at their feet. She shivered into her jacket as her eyes adjusted to the light. They got on board and Lex started up the engine. The boat stayed close to the shore as it cut through the darkened waters, past shadowy islands and glaciers.

As she glanced at him in the dim boat light,

she couldn't help but notice the frown lines between his eyes.

"You okay?" she asked eventually. "You look worried."

He shrugged. "I just don't want to let you all down."

"Oh, don't worry, you won't," she said. "You've never let me down."

She'd said the words lightly, hoping to sound reassuring and break the thick tension that seemed to fill the night air. But his frown deepened.

"You weren't disappointed when you found out that I'd gone to an Alaskan trooper's recruitment event and your boss recommended I stick with being a park ranger?" he asked. He still wasn't meeting her gaze.

"No…of course not. Lorenza clearly saw that you're great at what you do. And I think everybody's really thankful you're a park ranger right now—I know I am."

Again, she was trying to sound lighthearted. But still, he didn't smile.

"Look," she said. "Do we need to talk this out? Because I'm sorry if I made you feel like I was disappointed in you or something. I guess I've always been really driven and pushed myself, and maybe that made me push you. But I never meant to make you feel less about it. I loved you and everything about having you in my life. You helped me be better and stronger than I ever was without you."

Again, he didn't answer. It was like he was having some internal argument with himself that he wasn't letting her in on. She prayed that whenever he did choose to open up, God would help her find the right words to say.

Silence fell between them again, and eventually the boat slowed as he pulled into an inlet and brought the boat to shore. Dense trees surrounded them, jagged rocks spread out underneath. They started up the slope on foot in the darkness as stealthily as they could, sticking close together with Lex leading the way and Stormy bringing up the rear. Lex's flashlight swung a low, slow beam across the slippery ground. The rocks by the water's edge gave way to scrub and then dense fir trees.

"See?" He gestured first to scuff marks on the ground and then patches of bark worn off the trees. "Bears have definitely been through this area. Unfortunately, we can't tell if they're the ones we're looking for."

She shuddered, remembering what it had been like to come face-to-face with the brown bear the day before. "Can you at least tell if they're friendly bears or unfriendly ones?"

Finally, she got him to crack a smile.

"Never met a friendly bear in the wild," he said. "Don't think bears are designed to be. Although I've spent time at the wildlife conservation center outside Anchorage. It's really extraordinary how they rehabilitate animals and return them to the wild. There's hope that if we find the first bear cub soon enough, and he's in good enough shape, they'll be able to take care of him and then return him to a full, natural life in the forest again."

And if everything worked out as they hoped right now, the cub's sister might never even be poached.

Finally, he stopped in front of what looked like just another cliffside, seemingly no different than countless others they'd passed. Lex shone his light over it, and she saw the shimmering iridescence of the walls of an ice cave cutting into the rock.

"The bears won't be living in this one," he said. "It's too shallow for their needs. But there are several deeper ones nearby that they might be in and if we stake out here we should be able to hear if anything happens in the surrounding area. And I'm not about to go around knocking on caves looking for sleeping bears inside."

She chuckled. "Probably wise."

One up-close-and-personal bear encounter had been enough for one trip. Carefully they stepped into the cave, set a waterproof tarp down against one wall and sat on it side by side. The cave walls were freezing to the touch. But Stormy lay her huge, fuzzy bulk over their feet, snuggling up against Poppy's legs, filling her with warmth. Lex's flashlight beam ran over the walls and she watched as they glimmered in shades of purple, blue and green. Then he switched the light off and pitch-black filled the space around them.

"Welcome to your first stakeout," Poppy murmured. "Although usually we're in a car or apartment building, nowhere this beautiful."

"Thank you." Lex's voice came from the darkness. "Now what?"

"Now, we wait and make boring small talk," she replied. "Stakeouts are a whole lot of boring suddenly followed by a short burst of excitement."

"Got it," Lex said.

They sat for an hour and then a second one, with whispered chatter in between long lapses of silence. She told him about being partnered with Stormy, the K-9 training they went through together, some of the cases they'd worked on and the unique challenges of living with a dog the size of a small pony. He told her about his marriage to Danny's mom, how Debra's life had been a mess and she'd needed him. He'd married her and then they'd had a baby in the hope it would fix things, but it hadn't. Then she could hear warmth fill his voice as he talked about being a father and how deeply he loved his son. They also reminisced about some of the good times they had together and some of the moments they'd thought were bad times but realized in retrospect weren't as big a deal as they'd thought they were.

After a while, she found her side brushing his and her head touching his shoulder, and finally his arm slipping around her. Eventually they saw the soft gray light of the world lighting outside the cave. She glanced at her watch. It was almost five in the morning.

"We give it one more hour and then we call it a bust and head back," she said.

"You seem very calm about the fact I could be totally wrong about this," Lex asked.

"Because I have complete faith in you," she said, "and nobody's right all the time."

"Yeah, but maybe I don't want to let you down, again."

"Again?" She turned toward him and felt his hand brush her back. "Yes, Lex you ended our relationship and broke my heart, because you didn't see our marriage working and you thought that's what was best for both of us. But when it came to being a solid, caring and reliable man, you never let me down. Sure you weren't always the best at picking up on minor stuff, but I knew you'd always be there for me if I really needed you." She pressed her lips together a long moment and debated how much more to say. Then again, she'd be leaving his life in a few hours. If she wasn't going to be fully honest with him now, she might never get the opportunity to. "I just never thought you believed in yourself. And I wondered if that's why you were so focused on helping everybody else instead of figuring out what you wanted in life."

He didn't answer for a long moment and she wondered if she'd said something wrong.

"I mean, clearly I was wrong to push you into becoming a trooper," she added quickly, "and maybe you are living your best life working here in Glacier Bay now."

"My mother thought I use to shrink myself to make other people happy because I wanted to avoid conflict," Lex confessed. "She was who I was talking to in that one-sided pocket dial conversation I accidentally left on your phone before we broke up."

Poppy gasped. "Gillian? I thought she liked me!"

"She loved you," Lex said. "She was disappointed when I didn't marry you. But she also knew that I didn't feel good enough for you and that it was keeping me from stepping up and being an equal partner, like you deserved. She said a marriage should feel like a strong partnership of equals, not one person feeling more or less than the other."

She swallowed a painful breath. "I'm so sorry," she choked out. "Did I make you feel that way?"

He reached for her hand and squeezed it a long moment.

"Not really," he said. "Not on purpose. You were just so good at everything. Like, with the wedding, you were so organized and on top of everything. You clearly didn't need my help. I felt like if I did try to get involved I was just going to mess things up, and when I did try to suggest things you'd tell me it was already sorted."

"If I'd known that wedding planning was making you feel that way, I'd have canceled everything and just eloped with you!" Poppy said. "I loved you, Lex. I thought you were the most amazing person I'd ever met and I really wanted to marry you."

"Well, I really loved you and wanted to marry you, too," Lex said. "Truth is, I didn't move out to Gustavus because I was finally stepping up and chasing some big dream. I wanted to get away from everything that reminded me of you."

"Really?" She felt her voice drop.

"Yeah." His voice dropped, too. "You were so incredible, and I just couldn't convince myself I was worthy of you. The fact you went for the K-9 trooper training program the moment we split and got accepted…it made me feel like I'd never catch up."

"A relationship is not a competition." She chuckled softly. "I'm never going to be you and you're never going to be me. I don't have your instinctual heart for those who are suffering. You love people better and stronger than anyone I've ever known. Sure, I might be better at budgeting or spreadsheets, but my life was so much better and richer for having a man with a heart like yours in it."

She leaned forward and felt his forehead brush against hers.

"I could never ask you to give up Stormy, your career and your team to stay here with me," Lex whispered, his voice husky.

"And I could never ask you to be anyone other than who you're called to be, either," Poppy said.

"I wish I knew the right thing to say right now," Lex admitted.

"Yeah, me, too."

Her hands slipped up around his neck, and his fingers brushed her face. For one long moment, she let herself kiss him as he kissed her back. And somehow, despite all the tender embraces they'd shared in the past, this one felt deeper, richer...stronger. It was the kind of kiss shared between two people who'd cared for each other profoundly, missed each other and wished there'd been a way to stay in each other's lives.

Stormy growled, a deep guttural warning sound. The fur stood on end at the back of her neck. Poppy and Lex pulled apart and leaped to their feet.

"What's up, Stormy? What do you sense?" Poppy asked her partner. Her hand slid to Stormy's back. She could feel the tension radiating through her. "Show me."

They followed the K-9 out of the cave, walking single file, pushing their way slowly through the trees in the pale predawn light. For a moment she didn't hear anything.

Then came the wail, high-pitched and terrified. The animal cry was so eerily similar to that of a crying infant that Poppy felt her heart seize in terror as Danny's face filled her mind.

Somewhere, a little baby bear cub was crying out in fear.

"They've got her!" Lex called.

Their footsteps quickened as other sounds greeted their ears. The mama bear was snarling. Voices were shouting and swearing. Then she heard the sound of gunfire and the snarling abruptly stopped.

She prayed she'd reach the baby bear cub in time.

Then the trees parted in front of them and there lying on the ground ahead of them was the mother bear. Her black fur was tinged with a silver-blue around the paws and belly. Red blood soaked her soft fur from the bullet wound in her chest. Poppy grabbed Stormy's collar with one hand as she felt Lex grab her other one. Her heart ached.

"There's nothing we can do," he said and she could hear his own internal pain filling his voice. "She won't make it long enough for us to get her help. And in the meantime a wounded bear can be extremely dangerous."

She blinked back tears. They hadn't been quick enough to save the mama bear. But they would not fail her baby girl...

They pressed onward. Determination and strength radiated through Stormy's tall form, her body strained forward as if wanting to run but holding herself back awaiting Poppy's command. Her ears were perked toward the cacophony of sounds ahead.

The poachers were just steps ahead of them now, and she knew without a doubt that Stormy wouldn't let the little cub down. The K-9 would protect the terrified animal, while Poppy and Lex took the poachers into custody, unmasked them and stopped this travesty once and for all.

A motor roared ahead as they reached a clearing. There was tiny cub trapped in a cage on the back of an ATV. The larger poacher in fatigues sat at the handlebars, with the thinner poacher behind him.

"Go!" the thin man shouted, and the vehicle sped up, leaving Lex and Poppy running behind it.

Poppy pulled her weapon, even as she knew she'd never be able to make the shot at that distance.

"We're never going to outrun them on foot!" Lex shouted.

"No, but Stormy can," Poppy said. She turned to her partner. "Stop them!"

Stormy woofed loudly and charged. Her body sprinted, faster and faster, toward the ATV with the tiny captured bear on the back. Within a moment, she'd pulled alongside them. Her teeth bared as her body leaped. The ATV swerved.

A shot rang out.

Stormy yelped. Her body twisted unnaturally in the air as she fell backward. The ATV drove off into the dawn with the captured cub. The wolfhound collapsed.

Stormy had been shot.

TWELVE

"Stay with me!" Lex shouted to the huge dog as he and Poppy eased Stormy from the back of his truck and into his arms. The dog's eyes were closed, and her breath was labored. Blood soaked through the plaid shirt he'd tied around her leg like a tourniquet. He stumbled up his walkway to the front door, taking the heavy bulk of the dog's full weight into his arms. "You're going to be okay. I promise!"

Stormy whimpered. *Thank You, God!* The wound seemed superficial, as far as bullet wounds went, and the dog was still conscious. Later, he was sure his back and arms would hit him with the full ache and strain of having picked up a dog that heavy off the ground, working with Poppy to carry her through the woods to the boat, speeding as fast as he dared back to the dock and then lifting Stormy again into the truck to drive her home. But for now, there was nothing but adrenaline pumping through his veins.

He would save Stormy. He would not let Poppy down.

He could hear prayers pouring from Poppy's lips for her K-9 partner as she ran beside the dog's head.

His mother threw the front door open before they even reached the porch.

"Will and I got your texts," Gillian said, quickly stepping aside to let them in. "I've got the table prepped and Will is upstairs watching Danny. What do you need?"

"She was shot once, in the right hind leg," he said. "She should be fine. It's just a surface wound. But we've just got to clean the wound and stitch it up or we're looking at infection."

Gillian's portable table, which she used for emergency first-aid house calls, was spread out beside the dining room table. He lay Stormy down on it and looked around. Her medicine bag was on the kitchen island.

"Stay by her head and keep talking to her," he told Poppy as he made a beeline for the sink. "I'm going to wash up. She's going to be fine."

"You're closing the wound yourself?" Poppy asked.

"We have to," he said. He yanked the tap to scalding hot and started to lather his hands. "Our town's usual veterinarian won't be back from visiting his grandchildren in Anchorage for at least a week. And the closest emergency vet is in Juneau. But Mom worked in an emergency room and I've done more than my fair share of emergency animal care as a park ranger."

Then he turned the tap off with his elbow and turned back to Poppy. His heart ached as he saw the depth of worry that pooled in her eyes. Tears glistened on the edges of her lashes.

"Trust me," he said. "I've got this. She's going to be fine."

"I know." A weak smile crossed her lips. "I trust you."

He swallowed hard and prayed he wouldn't let her down.

"What can I do to help?" Poppy asked. She was pacing back and forth so quickly she was practically shaking. "What if Danny wakes up and hears us and it scares him? What should I tell my team? How is this going to affect her ability to be in the K-9 unit?"

"Poppy, listen to me," Lex said softly. Her visible agitation faded, and she stopped walking as he said her name. "You don't need to plan or be in charge of anything right now. You definitely don't need to worry. What I need you to do is be there for Stormy. Stay by her face and keep her calm. Cradle her head, stroke her nose, talk to her and pray for her. Reassure her that she's not alone and that she doesn't need to be scared, because you're there for her, okay?"

Poppy nodded. "Okay."

He took a deep breath, met his mother's eyes and then turned to where Stormy lay on the table.

Help me, Lord. Guide my hands. Then all distractions of the world around him faded as he focused on the task in front of him. It wasn't until after he'd stitched up Stormy's wound and carefully bandaged it again, and his mother had gone upstairs to check on Danny, that the ambient sounds of the world around him came back into focus.

He stepped back and Poppy's hopeful eyes met his.

"It's done," he said, his voice feeling oddly husky in his throat. "She's good. Really good. She might have a limp for a week, but I wouldn't be surprised if she's up and walking in a couple of hours. When you get back to Anchorage be sure to have her checked out by the K-9 vet. Now, come on, help me get her over to the blankets on the floor by the fire."

Poppy nodded and her eyes glistened. When she opened her mouth as if to speak, no words came out. Gently they carried Stormy over and laid her on the soft nest of blankets on the floor in front of the fire. He went back to the kitchen area to wash his hands and tidy up, and when he returned he found Poppy crouched on the ground beside her partner. She ran her hand gently over the back of Stormy's head. The wolfhound's eyes opened and her tongue licked Poppy's hand, then she closed her eyes again.

"Hey." Will's voice came from the doorway behind them. Lex turned. Poppy's colleague was standing there with his K-9 partner, Scout, by his side.

"Hey!" Poppy replied. She started to get up but Will waved her back down.

"Just wanted to let you know that I just got off the phone with Lorenza," he said. "She wants me to catch an early flight to Juneau to liaise with the team there. They don't know if the ship has left yet for the animal auction or not, but judging by the time you say the second bear was poached, they think we're dealing with a pretty small window of time. She said for you to call her later and she'll arrange a flight out for you and Stormy this afternoon."

"Thanks," Poppy replied.

"How's she doing?" Will asked. Concern filled his face.

"Pretty good," Poppy said, glancing back at her K-9 partner. "Thanks to Lex."

Will nodded and went upstairs, leaving them alone again. Lex crossed the room and sat down on the floor beside Poppy. She leaned back against him, and he wrapped his arms around her shoulders from behind.

"How soon until you think she can fly home?" Poppy asked.

"Few hours," Lex said. "Not long. She really is a tough dog."

"She is." Poppy nodded, and he felt her soft hair against his face.

"I'm sorry we didn't stop the other bear cub from being poached."

She turned and looked over her shoulder at him. Her cheek brushed against his arm. "Are you kidding?" she asked. "You were completely right about the location. If anything, it's my fault for telling Stormy to charge into danger like that, but that's her job. She's a state trooper and is trained to risk her life when duty requires her to. Stormy's far more than just a dog. She's a law enforcement officer."

"I know," Lex said softly.

Just as he knew there was absolutely no way to relieve the unrelenting heaviness inside his heart. Here Poppy was in his arms, her face just inches from his. It would take nothing to lean forward, kiss her lips and pull her closer. But then what? There was little he could say. There was no way he could ever ask her to give up her partner, her career and her team to move here to Gustavus to start a life with him and Danny, no matter how much his heart might want to. There was no possible compromise where she somehow kept her job with the K-9 trooper unit and lived somewhere so remote she'd have to fly hours to every case. And if he gave up his life here to chase after her, wouldn't he just be repeating a new variation of the mistakes he'd made in the past?

"I'm really going to miss you," Poppy whispered.

She closed her eyes and as his hand brushed the side of her face he felt the soft wetness of tears slipping from underneath her eyelids.

"Me, too," he said.

His heart lurched. He wanted to be her hero, to swing into action and rescue her from the situation they were in. He wanted to go back in time and fix their past heartbreak. He wanted to solve the case, capture the poachers, rescue the glacier bear cubs and rehabilitate them back into the wild himself.

Maybe he'd always wanted to be the one to leap in and rescue her, on some level, and when he didn't need to he didn't know what role he was supposed to play in her life. *A marriage should feel like a strong partnership of equals.* He had no idea what that would even look like.

All he knew is that the longer he stayed there, holding Poppy in his arms and wiping her tears from her eyes, the more likely he was to pull her close, kiss her lips and hand her his damaged heart.

Then they'd both end up hurt again. For both their sakes, he couldn't let that happen.

"I've got to go," he said, easing himself away from her and standing. "I'm sorry, I have to get to work. Glacier Bay National Park opens to tourists for the season in about two weeks and we've still got a lot to do to get it ready. Not to mention we have to manage the press side of the bear cubs being poached."

She looked up at him for a long moment, then she stood and ran her hands through her hair.

"Yeah, you're right," she said. "I'm sorry, I guess I forgot you've got more to your job than just escorting us around and helping out my team."

A forced smile crossed her face and he recognized it in an instant as the one she used when she was determined to put a bright spin on things instead of falling apart.

"Depending when you get back, I might not be here," she added. "I know that Will definitely won't be as he's leaving momentarily by the sound of things. But until I talk to Lorenza, I won't know when they're flying me out."

Yeah, she was definitely using that upbeat tone of voice that meant she'd decided not to be upset. It was one he wished he'd paid more attention to in the past, before it was too late.

"I'm probably looking at a ten-or twelve-hour workday today, to be honest," he said, hoping his attempt to be positive sounded as natural as hers. He shifted his weight from one foot to another. "There's not much I can do to help with the case now that the bears have been poached, and I've got a lot of overtime ahead of me to catch up on everything. But text or call me to let me know when you're leaving, okay? And if you happen to still be here tonight when I get back, maybe you can let me know how things are going with the case?"

Poppy gasped, her attention suddenly diverted before she could answer, and it took a moment to figure out why. He turned. Stormy was slowly climbing to her feet. They watched as she rose, gingerly at first, testing whether to put weight on her bandaged hind leg before deciding against it and standing on three. Her tail thumped weakly. Prayers of thanksgiving slipped almost silently from Poppy's lips.

"You're up," Lex said. He reached out his hand and Stormy licked it gently. "You really are something else. Even injured you can probably still beat me at crawling."

"I'm sorry." Will's voice came from behind them. "Your mom's on a phone call. And I tried to stop him, but he got away from me."

Lex turned and there stood Danny still in his pajamas, holding the kitten in front of him with both hands.

"Grandma said Stormy hurt," Danny said. "Mu'shoom want help!"

Poppy's hand rose to her lips as if to stifle a cry as Danny crossed the floor carefully holding the kitten.

"No problem," Lex told Will.

The trooper walked over to the kitchen and poured some food in a bowl for Scout and an instant later his K-9 partner bounded down the stairs to join him.

With Lex's guiding hand, Danny set Mushroom down beside Stormy. The wolfhound bent down and sniffed the kitten's head, then slowly she eased herself back to lying down. The kitten curled up against her snout and Stormy's tail thumped slowly in response.

Lex swept Danny up into his arms. "That was very good thinking, buddy."

"Good kitten," Danny said.

"Yes," Poppy replied. "She's not big and strong like Stormy, but she's very good at being a kitten. And you are very good at being you."

Danny nodded enthusiastically and Lex cuddled his son closely.

"I'm going to hug you both now," Poppy said. "This seems like a good time to say goodbye."

She stepped forward and wrapped her arms around both of them at once. For a long moment he felt her there, holding on to both him and his son, before she pulled away.

"I am so happy that I came here to see you and your daddy," she told Danny brightly. "You are so wonderful and thank you so much for inviting me into your house."

"Stormy come back?" Danny asked.

Lex watched as Poppy's smile wavered slightly, but all she said was, "That is a great idea."

He swallowed a painful breath. "Take care of yourself, Poppy. Don't forget to let me know how Stormy is and that you made it home safe."

"Will do. Bye, Lex."

"Bye, Poppy."

Then he turned, walked out of the room and carried his son upstairs, feeling the hopeless weight of regret in every step.

Poppy exhaled. So, that was that, then. She and Lex had opened another chapter, only to close it, leaving her with the new ache in her heart just as painful as the old one.

Lord, I want to fix this mess, but I don't know how. I've always believed, on some level, that if only I worked hard enough and tried hard enough I could make anything happen. And now? I'm realizing how wrong I was to think I could ever make a relationship with Lex work all on my own. I wish we'd been genuine partners.

"Hey." Will's voice drew her attention back to the room. He was still standing in the kitchen with Scout by the dog bowls. She'd forgotten he was there. "Why don't you go lie down for a bit? I'm guessing you haven't slept. Scout and I can keep an eye on Stormy for you. I've got a can of some really great wet food I save for special occasions in my bag, and I'm sure Scout would be happy to share it with Stormy."

"Thank you," Poppy said, not that she had any confidence her weary heart and body would be able to sleep. "When do you head out?"

"Little over half an hour."

"See you, then." She gave Stormy one more scratch behind the ears, then bent down and kissed the top of her partner's shaggy gray head. Then Poppy went into her room, kicked off the boots she'd forgotten to take off when she'd rushed into the house with a wounded Stormy and lay on top of the bed, fully clothed. Despite what she'd been expecting, she passed out into a deep and dreamless sleep almost immediately, before she could even formulate prayers in her exhausted mind.

Poppy awoke to find the door ajar and Stormy sleeping on the floor beside her bed. She checked her phone and saw with a jolt that over two hours had passed. There was a text from Will telling her that when he'd come to say goodbye, she'd been sleeping so soundly he'd let her be and would see her soon. Another message from Lorenza told her to give her a shout when she woke up, which Poppy guessed meant Will had told her she was napping.

She freshened up and headed out into the living room, Stormy slowly walking on three legs behind her. There she found a note on the kitchen island from Gillian letting her know that she and Danny had gone to see friends, and Lex was at work, but that she'd left Poppy food in the fridge. She glanced at the front door and found it locked.

"Okay, then," she said to Stormy, "guess it's just you and me, partner."

She texted Lorenza that she was awake and

free to chat. Moments later her laptop rang with a phone call from Eli. Poppy sat down at the table and Stormy lay beside her and rested her head on Poppy's leg. She answered the call and blinked to see almost the entire K-9 team's smiling faces in boxes on the screen.

"Hi!" she said, running her hands through her hair. Her eyes flickered around the screen.

All of the troopers were there, except for Sean and Gabriel, who she guessed were off searching for the survivalist family, and Will, who she presumed was still in transit. Lorenza's assistant, Katie, was there, too, sharing a screen with tech guru Eli.

"I'm sorry, did I miss a team meeting?" Poppy asked.

"Just a bit," Eli said with a grin.

"But don't worry about it," Lorenza added quickly. "You're allowed to rest, especially after everything you've been through. How's Stormy? Do you think she'll be up to flying back to Anchorage at three?"

Poppy looked over to where her partner lay in a sunbeam by the back window. The wolfhound snored slightly.

"Yeah, I think so," she answered. "She's up and walking already, but she's taking it very slow."

"Wonderful." Lorenza smiled. "Well, wish her the best from all of us and rest assured that we'll have a vet ready to check her out when she gets back."

"Any update on the poached bear cubs or the animal auction ship yet?" Poppy asked.

"Sadly, no," Lorenza said. "But we're expecting Will to check in soon after he coordinates with the coast guard team on the ground in Juneau. And, of course, Eli is working double-time to try and locate this boat from every possible angle. We'll find those bears and bring them home to Alaska. Meanwhile, Helena was just giving us an update on the missing bride case and her interview with the groom Lance's sister, Tessa."

"Thank you again, Poppy, for giving me your perspective on how your interviews for this case had gone," Helena said. "You were right, there's definitely more there worth looking into and I can see why Lance's ex-girlfriend suggested we talk to Tessa to get a different viewpoint than the rosy one his parents were painting."

"So, she backed up Lance's ex-girlfriend's story?" Poppy asked.

"Yes and more so," Helena said. "To hear Tessa tell it, her brother is a raging narcissist and a liar who's really good at fooling people into seeing whatever side of him they want him to see. She says he was never able to fool her because they grew up together so she saw the kind of stuff he pulled and what he got away with."

"Wow," Poppy murmured. "Although, to be honest, I'm not surprised, considering how much Lance's ex-girlfriend wanted us to talk to her."

"According to Tessa, anything Lance tells us should be discounted and flipped on its head," Helena added. Then she frowned. "But sibling relationships are complicated. I've got a fraternal twin who's made some bad choices herself."

"All the more reason to bring Lance and his best man, Jared, in for questioning again," Lorenza said. "Anyone got anything else?"

Brayden waved a hand.

"Not sure if it counts as progress," the trooper said, "but another reindeer went missing from the sanctuary."

"Apparently, my aunt blamed one of the farm hands," Katie chimed in. "He got so mad about it that he quit. She's really at her wits' end about who's behind this."

"Do you think Lex would mind if I picked

his brain sometime?" Brayden added. "It sounded like he knew a lot about the animal rehabilitation community."

"I'm sure he'd be happy to," Poppy said. She debated mentioning her complicated past with Lex, but wasn't quite sure where to start. She didn't doubt that when she was ready to talk it out with someone her team would be there for her, and for that she was thankful. An odd thought crossed her mind. "Katie, have you tried looking into people you and your aunt have been romantically involved with? It's like what Helena said about how sibling relationships are complicated—romantic relationships are, too."

A light dawned behind Katie's eyes. "It's worth a shot. I'll start working on a list."

"I'll help you," Brayden said.

Motion drew her eyes to the front window. There was someone standing on the porch. Then the doorknob rattled, like someone was trying to let themselves in but couldn't get the door unlocked.

"Hang on," Poppy said, and stood. "I think there's someone at the door."

She muted the call, left her laptop on the living room table, walked to the front entrance and glanced through the curtains. It was Ripley, standing on the porch in a T-shirt, long sweater and pair of plaid pajama-style pants that looked too thin for the spring chill in the air. Her arms were crossed so tightly her hands to be seemed wedged under her arms.

Poppy opened the door.

"Ripley!" she said. "Hi! What are you doing here?"

And had she just been trying to let herself in?

"Is Lex home?" Ripley asked. The younger woman's gaze darted to Poppy's face for a moment and then back to the ground, but not before Poppy noticed the raccoon rings of day-old makeup smudged by tears in her eyes.

"No," Poppy said. "But do you want to come in? I was about to make some coffee and you could join me for a late brunch."

Ripley hesitated.

"I can't stay long," she said. "My brother Nolan dropped me off, and he'll be back soon."

"Is everything okay?" Poppy asked.

"No, I mean yeah," Ripley said. "I'm fine. I just wanted to thank Lex for everything and let him know we're leaving town for a bit. I just need to get away for a while."

Poppy believed that last statement, but she wasn't sure about the rest.

"Well, come inside and I'll give Lex a call to let him know you're here," Poppy said and stepped back. "I'm just finishing up a video call with my team, then we can chat while you wait for Lex. Nolan's very welcome to join us too when he gets back."

In fact, she very much hoped he would. It was about time she got to the bottom of what was going on. Ripley unfolded slightly as she stepped into the warmth, and Poppy closed the door behind her. The young woman's hand darted toward her pocket but not before Poppy's keen eyes caught a glimpse of the keychain in her hands.

"Did Johnny give you a set of Lex's house keys?" Poppy asked. "I thought Lex asked Johnny to give those back."

And apparently he'd made a spare copy before he had. She reached out her hand expectantly with her palm open. The keys shook as Ripley dropped the keys into them.

"Yeah," she said, her eyes darting everywhere but Poppy's face. "He said that Lex was a really good man and that if I was ever in trouble or I needed help I could come here, and Lex would make sure I was okay."

Poppy felt both her heart and mind swirling with questions like two water wheels working together to try and sift lies from truth. Yes, she could see Johnny making a secret copy of Lex's house keys if he thought Ripley was in danger and might need a place to hide. Did that mean that he was also the one who boobytrapped his own house?

She took a deep breath and prayed for wisdom.

"I need to quickly finish my video call," she said. "But then I'm looking forward to talking with you while we wait for Lex. I'm really glad you came over, especially if you were worried about something. You're safe here."

Ripley nodded weakly, then she stood almost hovering in the living room doorway as Poppy picked up her laptop and took it into the bedroom.

"I've got an unexpected visitor," Poppy said to her team as she restarted the call. "Johnny's girlfriend is here. She was actually trying to let herself in with a copy of the keys Lex gave him."

Helena sucked in a sharp breath. "Do you think that's where the guy who broke in and tried to kidnap Danny got his keys from too?"

"I can't rule that out," Poppy said. "She says her brother dropped her off and will be back to pick her up in a bit. I'm just really thankful she's here. Hopefully, she'll open up to me and we'll finally get some answers."

"If anyone can get through to her you can," Lorenza said.

The video call ended in a flurry of good-byes from both her team and a scattering of their K-9 partners who made brief appearances on the screens. She dialed Lex's cell-phone number, and when he didn't answer left a voicemail message saying Ripley was at the house. Then she headed back into the living room.

Ripley was nowhere to be seen. Stormy looked up at Poppy from where the dog lay on the floor.

Poppy glanced at Stormy. "Where did she go?"

The wolfhound whined softly. A soft thud came from the floor above her, followed by the sound of several somethings clattering on the floor. She turned, ran upstairs and raced down the hall, just in time to see Ripley dashing away down the stairs in the opposite direction. She'd taken her sweatshirt off and was now clutching it to her chest like there was something bundled inside it. A passing glimpse into Gillian's room showed what looked like the contents of the woman's jewelry case strewn across the floor.

She'd been robbing them?

"Ripley!" Poppy shouted. "Stop!"

She pelted after her, down the stairs, as Ripley burst through the back door and out onto the lawn. The door slammed shut behind her, leaving Stormy behind on the other side. Poppy didn't have her weapon on her but could easily outrun and tackle the frailer woman.

"I'm giving you to the count of three!" Poppy shouted. "One, two—"

Ripley stopped so suddenly that Poppy almost barreled into her. The young woman turned and raised her hands, dropping the sweatshirt and sending even more jewelry and a mason jar full of loose coins and bills spilling onto the grass.

"I'm sorry!" Ripley's voice quivered. "I need money. I was hoping Lex would lend me some. But when he wasn't here…"

For a long beat Poppy just stared at her, knowing that Ripley was aware she'd been caught red-handed and asking God's wisdom in what to do next. Yes, she could arrest her and probably still would. But, if she showed the woman mercy, would God use it to open up Ripley's heart? Then Poppy saw the small, round bruises on Ripley's forearms, the telltale signs that someone had grabbed her arms roughly and held on to her too tight.

It was only then she realized she still hadn't called Lex. If only he were here...

"What do you need money for, Ripley?" she asked. "I heard your ex-boyfriend Kevin was back in town saying something about you owing him money. Is he the one who left those bruises on your arms?"

"Like I told everybody, Kevin left town days ago," Ripley said almost mechanically as if repeating something she'd been told to say. "Nolan flew him out of town right before Johnny died."

But those bruises weren't a few days old.

"Was it your brother, Nolan?"

"No!" Ripley's voice rose as something bordering on indignation flashed in her eyes. "Nolan would never hurt me. He's only ever wanted to protect me!"

Fair enough, that much Poppy believed. But during her time in law enforcement Poppy had seen far too many people make very bad decisions to protect others.

"Is Kevin the one who locked you in the closet and killed Johnny?" she asked, gently.

"I don't know." Ripley's lip quivered "He was masked…"

"But you think it could be," Poppy said. Ripley nodded. "I can't give you money, and I definitely can't let you rob Gillian and Lex. But I want to help you and I'm willing to listen. How about I gather up these things, we go back inside and talk?"

Before she could answer, a large black truck pulled up down the road and stopped beside the house. The man behind the wheel was big, with hands too big and beefy to have left those bruises. A handgun sat on the dashboard just within reach. Between his beard and baseball cap his face was pretty well covered. But something about his form sent a chill down her spine.

Ripley's brother, Nolan, was the large poacher.

But how? Will had been convinced Nolan was protective of Ripley and would never hurt her.

Nolan leaned over and threw the door open for his sister.

"Get in!" he shouted. "We've got to go."

The sound of the man's voice confirmed it.

This man was one of the criminals behind everything that had happened and the only one who could help them stop the sale of the bear cubs. She couldn't let him take Ripley and leave. But her weapon was still in her room, Stormy was injured, her team was hours away and she had no backup. She was on her own.

Then an idea struck her.

She reached into her pocket for her phone and hit redial, praying Lex would pick up.

"But, she knows about Kevin," Ripley said. "If we tell her what's happening, maybe she can help us."

"Or maybe we all end up dead." Nolan's eyes narrowed. His hand twitched toward his gun. "This only ends one way. So, Poppy, mind your own business if you know what's good for you. Ripley, get in the truck."

THIRTEEN

Lex's phone was ringing again as he pulled back into his parking space in front of the lodge after a tour of the park's cabins to see which ones were still in need of repair. He turned off the engine, undid his seat belt and glanced at the screen. It was Poppy, again. Lex had let the call go through to voice mail the first time, figuring she was just calling to let him know about her flight home to Anchorage. He'd been mentally kicking himself for letting her go yet again, while also not knowing how he could possibly keep her in his life in any meaningful way, and hearing the sound of her voice was just a little more than he was up for right in that moment.

But now the fact she was calling a second time within a few minutes worried him.

Lord, guide my words and help me be wise

in what I say and do. I care about this woman so much. But I only want her in my life and by my side if I can do it right.

He answered on the third ring.

"Hey, Poppy," he said. "How's it going?" She didn't answer. For a moment he heard nothing but background noise of trees rustling, voices too muffled to understand and fabric shuffling. "Hello? Poppy?"

Still nothing. His head shook. Unbelievable, she'd apparently pocket-dialed him. He reached to hang up the phone when he heard Poppy's voice cutting loudly through the sound.

"Ripley," she said. "I don't think you should get into the truck with Nolan. I think we should go back inside the bed-and-breakfast and call Lex."

He froze, his finger still reaching for the button, then he leaned back against the front seat of his truck.

"Poppy? I'm here." He raised his voice. "Can you hear me?"

She didn't answer and he suspected she'd either muted the call or his voice was muffled by her phone being in his pocket.

Nolan's voice rose. "Get in the truck. Now."

"Ripley, listen to me," Poppy said, her

voice urgent. "I know Johnny loved you and wouldn't want to see you hurt. It's clear from the bruises on your arm that someone's been rough with you. I'm guessing it was Kevin and that you both have been lying about him leaving town."

Lex knew without a doubt that he was the true audience of her words. His heart ached, knowing she probably didn't even know for certain that he could hear her.

Poppy, I'm here. I'm listening.

"That's enough!" Nolan's voice bellowed.

A gun clicked. Lex's breath froze in his chest. He grabbed his keys, fired up the engine and threw his truck in Reverse.

Hang on, Poppy, I'm coming.

"Ripley, I think Kevin came to town when he got out of jail to cause trouble for you and didn't leave," Poppy's words tumbled over each other quickly, as if she knew she was running out of time to speak them. "I'm guessing he somehow forced your brother into helping him poach baby bears. Maybe he said it would settle the score between you. Or that he'd finally leave Ripley alone if he did. I know he told people you owed him money. You got worried for your brother, or for yourself, and told Johnny who told Lex. But instead Kevin killed Johnny."

"Not another word!" Nolan's voice rose to a roar. "Hands up where I can see them!"

"Lex!" Poppy shouted. "Help! I'm—"

A gun fired. The phone went dead.

"Poppy!" Lex shouted, feeling her name wrenched from somewhere deep inside his heart. "Lord, please, you've got to help me save her!"

He hit Redial as he drove as fast as he dared back through the trees toward Gustavus. Nobody answered. He called his mother and told her Poppy was in trouble, to keep Danny safe and stay with friends. The second he heard her agree he hung up and called Will. The trooper didn't answer. He tried Poppy's line again. It rang through to voice mail.

Lord, help me. I don't know what's going on. I don't know where she is. All I know is that she's in danger and she needs me to save her. I can't let her down.

Finally, he reached his home and swerved into the driveway, barely stopping the engine before he leaped out. The glass on the road in front of his house told him a vehicle window had been shot. Flattened grass indicated there'd been a struggle.

He ran up to the house, threw open the door and ran inside. It was deserted and untouched. Poppy was gone. Then he heard the sound of barking rise around him as, moments later, Stormy scrambled down the hall faster than he'd have dreamed imaginable considering her injury and butted hcr head against his leg.

"Poppy's gone, isn't she?" He ran his hand along the K-9's head. "Don't worry. We're going to find her."

He found her laptop on the table and turned it on. As the screen came to life, he tried the same password she'd used back when they were dating to stream movies on her television and breathed a prayer of thanks when it worked. Then he took a breath, opened the video chat call and hit the one for Colonel Lorenza Gallo.

Moments later the head of the K-9 unit appeared on screen. She blinked.

"Lex?" she said. "Where's Poppy?"

"She's been kidnapped," he informed her. "By Nolan who also has his sister with him and might have kidnapped her, too. I need help."

Lorenza's face paled.

"I'm sending a team immediately," Lorenza said, her hands moving rapidly over the keyboard. "But they won't get there for over an hour."

Over an *hour*? Poppy might not have that long.

"Where did he take her?" Lorenza asked.

"I don't know!" He tried to sit but found himself jumping right back up again. "The docks, I'm guessing. But I don't know which one or which direction they went to meet up with that boat your team is searching for. There are multiple ways to leave the glaciers and so many places they could hide."

"Think," Lorenza said, her tone so firm it was almost a command. "Poppy's counting on you right now. She's all you've got to direct us where to go."

He felt Stormy's head drop onto his knee. The wolfhound looked up at him and he ran his hand along her back. They were all Poppy had, a wounded K-9 dog and a park ranger who struggled with self-doubt.

"Where is she?" Lorenza's voice cut through his thoughts.

"I told you... I don't know!"

"Take a deep breath," Lorenza said. "Hold

it for three seconds. Then let it out and start telling me everything you *do* know."

He took a deep breath in, praying for God's guidance, then let it out again.

"When she called me, she was with Ripley and Nolan," Lex said. "It sounded like Nolan was trying to take Ripley somewhere."

"Did she mention a boat?" Lorenza asked.

"No, just his truck. But she speculated that Kevin somehow forced Nolan into helping him poach the bear. She guessed maybe it was because he thought they owed him money or maybe he promised to leave Ripley alone if he did. She also speculated that Ripley had been the one who'd told Johnny about the bears."

Of course. His former friend was nothing if not loyal and had lied about going to the watering hole to protect the woman he loved. Lex just wished he'd seen it sooner.

"I know all the web traffic says the bear cubs were being moved by boat," Lex added, "but that doesn't make sense considering Nolan owns a small charter airline. I'm guessing Kevin is the one who tried to take Danny hostage. And if he was telling the truth about already having a client lined up to take the cubs, as Poppy suspected, maybe the whole boat business thing online is a red herring.

Could be that there is no overseas animal auction and no ship. Which means that it was just a ruse to draw attention away from Nolan's remote airfield."

He closed his eyes a moment and when he opened them again he felt a fresh surge of adrenaline fill his core.

"Nolan had to have taken her to his airfield," he said. "It's just a guess but an educated one based on Poppy's theory that what Danny's kidnapper said was the truth, not the online posting. And that has already turned out to be partially right."

'Good enough for me," Lorenza told him. "I'll send Will back from Juneau, with backup, to meet you there."

"I'm taking Stormy with me," he said. "I know she's limping and can't leap into action, but she's my best hope for sniffing out where they have Poppy stashed if they've hidden her somewhere."

The wolfhound looked up at him and he knew that the K-9 wouldn't have had it any other way.

He just hoped they reached her in time.

Poppy woke up to find her head groggy, what felt like a bandanna blindfolding her eyes and her hands tied together behind her back with plastic zip ties.

Just like she'd found Johnny.

Please, God, help me focus. She was sitting on what felt like a wooden chair. Despite the fact her eyes were blindfolded, the brightness of the light shining through the thin layer of fabric let her know it was still daytime and probably even still late morning. The combination of brain fog and a twinge in her neck told her she'd been sedated with something sharp, probably a dart, but she could also tell it hadn't been that strong. Poppy raised her head and blinked, scrunching her face just enough to catch a glimpse of the world underneath a tiny gap in the bottom of her blindfold. She couldn't see much, not much more than a sliver. But it was enough to tell she was on a concrete floor with crates stacked high on the edges of the room, like in some kind of warehouse. Then she caught a sliver of blue sky to her right.

She was in an airplane hangar.

Help me, Lord, nobody knows I'm here! The entire might of the K-9 trooper unit was focused on checking the harbors, ports and ocean beyond for boats, and here Nolan had taken her to his small private airport.

Sounds reached her ears now, mingling with the beat of her own heart pounding. Multiple voices were talking over each other in a garbled mass of sound. There were at least three men, by the sounds of it, and it sounded like they were arguing over money being exchanged and some kind of big financial deal was going down. There was a low growling too that sent shivers of danger down her spine. Then she heard the plaintive sound of two baby bear cubs crying and realized their sale was happening here and now.

And she was a helpless witness to it—kidnapped, alone and unable to do anything to stop it but pray.

Then she heard another noise coming from behind her. It was a rustling so subtle she could barely make it out above the chaos of noises swirling in front of her. But she heard it nonetheless, a low and soft sound like someone was crawling through crates and tarps across the floor toward her.

No... It couldn't be.

A warm furry head brushed against her bound hands and a wet tongue licked her fingertips.

"Stormy!" She whispered her partner's name so softly it was almost silent on her lips, but she knew the dog's excellent hearing would pick it up. "Good girl."

What was her injured partner doing here? Let alone crawling across the floor like she'd demonstrated in the bed-and-breakfast to make Danny giggle in what felt like a lifetime ago?

But then she felt the dog shift so that her fingers brushed the K-9 canvas harness that Stormy was now somehow dressed in and felt something cold and hard underneath her fingertips. She eased it out of the harness.

It was a pocketknife. Tears rose in her eyes. *Oh, Lex. You're here, too?* He'd found her, and instead of charging into danger and risking their lives to help her, he'd sent Stormy to arm her.

"Good girl," she whispered again. "Now go and hide! Stormy, hide!"

She pressed her lips together and prayed her partner would obey her command. Then something lurched in her chest as she felt the dog's soft fur leave her touch and heard the sound of Stormy crawling away. She turned the knife slowly in her bound fingertips, pricking her thumb slightly as she released the blade and slid it between the plastic zip ties. Then she began cutting. Relief flooded her limbs as she felt the bonds loosening. Just a couple more moments and she'd be able to snap them free.

A crash sounded somewhere behind her and to her left like a box toppling over.

"What was that?" called the skinny poacher, who she now assumed was Kevin. "Go check it out."

Fear seized her. Was it Stormy? Was it Lex?

She stopped cutting, hid the knife in her hands and started shaking the chair from left to right, banging the wooden legs on the concrete as loudly as she could to draw all eyes and attention to her.

"She's awake!" Nolan shouted.

"Go get her to stop!" Kevin replied.

Her distraction worked well enough. She heard footsteps pounding toward her.

"Stop that!" Nolan bellowed. "Right now!"

She complied. The poacher's feet stopped just inches to her right, so close she could see his knees and boots through the thin gap at the bottom of the blindfold.

"Listen," Nolan hissed as he leaned closer. "This whole thing is almost done, okay? In just a few more minutes, the buyer will leave with the bears, Kevin will get his money, we'll let you go and we can all go on with our lives."

His voice was so earnest it pained her to think just how much he needed to believe it was true.

"Where's your sister?" she whispered.

"Waiting in the truck," he said.

"Is she free to go or did Kevin insist she was tied up?" Poppy hazarded a guess.

The fact he didn't answer told her everything she needed to know.

"This is just about money," Nolan said. "Kevin won't leave Ripley alone until he gets the money he thinks we owe him for lawyer's fees, bail and losing his business and stuff, from when we called the police on him and he went to jail. You were right, okay? He said if I helped him poach and sell the cubs we'd be even. Then he'd leave Ripley alone and never bother her again."

"You figured if calling the police on him and even sending him to jail didn't keep him away, you'd step up and fix it, right?" Poppy whispered. "I get that. But it won't work. He'll just keep coming back."

"Hey!" Kevin snapped from what sounded like the other side of the hangar. "What are you doing over there? I didn't give you permission to start chatting with her. What's she saying? Tell me what she's telling you!"

Poppy risked sliding the blade of the knife back between her bound wrists again.

"Just shut up, okay?" Nolan whispered. "Or he's going to make me knock you out again and I don't want to."

"Let me go," Poppy whispered back. "I'll save Ripley and protect her. I promise."

Nolan hesitated.

"Change of plans!" Kevin shouted. "The client doesn't want the brown bear. Says it's too big for their little plane. Plus he's worried it's gonna wake up and if we tranq it again, its heart might stop. But he likes the look of Poppy and is willing to pay extra to take her, too. We got the cubs on the plane already and his pilot is all fueled up and ready to go. Help me get the girl on the plane for him quick and then we're done."

Her heart stopped as a quiver of fear sent chills through her core. But she gritted her teeth and prayed.

Lord, give me the strength I need to escape this evil.

"Time for you to choose whether you're going to be a hero or a villain, Nolan," Poppy said. She wrenched her hands apart, her wrist screaming in pain as the bonds snapped. Then, leaping from the chair, she yanked the blindfold down with one hand and clenched the knife in the other.

Sunlight flooded her eyes. Out of her periphery, she saw Kevin dash out the wide and open side of a modest airplane hangar toward what looked like a small but very expensive private plane. She spun toward Nolan.

"I'm Trooper Poppy Walsh of the Alaska K-9 Unit and you're under arrest for poaching, kidnapping, murder and attempted murder. You have the right to remain silent—"

"You kidding me?" He gripped his gun with both hands and pointed it at her face. "I've got a gun aimed at you, and all you've got is a little knife!"

"Yeah," Poppy agreed. "But you're alone and I've got backup."

Somewhere. She couldn't see Lex or hear him. She had no proof that she wasn't alone and that there was no one hiding among the boxes and crates to leap out and save her.

But she knew Lex and that was all she needed to know.

"Now," she said. "Drop your weapon and get down with your hands up."

Nolan hesitated, the small private engine

began to purr and Kevin leaned back in and shouted, "Just shoot her in the leg already and we'll drag her!"

Nolan shook his head as if arguing with himself and aimed his weapon at her leg. The sound of a bullet fired, cracking the air. As she watched, Nolan dropped his gun and clutched his shoulder, screaming in pain as the unseen marksman took out his arm before he could even fire.

"Put pressure on it," Lex shouted. He sprinted out from behind a wall of crates with his gun in his hand. "A tourniquet would be great. You'll need a few stitches, but you'll be fine. We're going to go save the bears and your sister."

Poppy yanked the clip from Nolan's weapon. "Then I'm arresting you."

Lex met her eyes and grinned, and she knew without a doubt that she'd give anything to see that strong, determined and charming smile every day for the rest of her life. He reached into his coat's inside pocket and pulled out her badge and weapon. "Thought you might need these."

"Thank you." She took them and then looked past him. "Where's Stormy?"

"My truck." He ran for the door and she

matched pace. "It's hidden around the corner. I thought she'd be safest there, so I snuck her back out after she brought the knife to you."

"Thank you," she said. "You know, you could've left her safe at home."

"You kidding? Stormy would've never forgiven me." She chuckled. Yeah, that was true. "Plus, I needed her tracking skills to find you."

They stepped out into the bright Alaskan sunlight, side by side. Poppy scanned the airfield and suddenly realized what Lex had meant about tracking her. Several small buildings, garages, hangars and sheds dotted the expansive plot of land, intersected by three different runways.

Far to their left, the private plane was driving down to the end of a runway preparing to take off, with the blue cubs inside. Nearby the brown bear lay on its side in a wooden storage crate far too flimsy for an animal its size. Its breathing was erratic, the tranquilizers were definitely wearing off and considering what it'd been through that bear would be likely to lash out and attack the first thing it saw the second it could.

Then a panicked scream for help dragged her attention to the right. Kevin was sitting in the front seat of Nolan's pickup truck, a terrified and bound Ripley beside him on the passenger seat.

"Shut up!" Kevin backhanded her across the face and gunned the engine.

Kevin was kidnapping Ripley. The little blue cubs were about to fly off with the client who'd paid for them to be trafficked. Another suffering and dangerous bear needed their help, as well.

No matter how hard she tried, she couldn't save them all.

She glanced at Lex, and as her eyes met his, she knew it wasn't even a question.

"We've got to stop that monster from taking Ripley," he said.

"Where's your truck?" she asked.

"This way!"

She followed him and they ran for a nearby shed, yanked the door open and sprinted inside. Stormy woofed in greeting from the front seat of Lex's truck, her voice filling the small space.

"I'll drive," Lex said.

"And I'll shoot," Poppy added. She yanked the passenger side door open and slid in beside her dog. "Stormy, get in the back."

The K-9 barked in agreement and complied. Lex gunned the engine and his truck shot out of the building and onto the runway. She glanced in the rearview mirror. The private plane was almost at the end of the runway. Then all it had to do was turn around and come back at speed for takeoff. She watched Lex's eyes follow the same path hers had taken.

Then he gripped the steering wheel tightly with both hands and fixed his gaze on Nolan's truck, with Kevin and Ripley inside.

"Hold on," he said. "I'm going to speed."

He gunned the engine and chased after the stolen truck, with Ripley still screaming for help inside. Poppy opened her window and braced her weapon to fire as Lex edged the truck closer and closer. Then he swerved sharply to the right, cutting as close to the truck as he dared. She leaned out the window, aimed for the back tire and fired. The rubber exploded with a bang and the truck spun, flying out of control so quickly that Lex had to mash the brakes to keep from driving into it.

Then, with the jarring sound of metal hitting wood, the truck slammed into a towering fir tree almost half its length. Kevin tumbled out and ran.

"I'll get Ripley," she shouted to Lex as

he yanked the door open. "Go take Kevin down!"

She allowed herself to watch for one fleeting moment as he sprinted after Kevin, launched at him in a football tackle and brought him to the ground. Poppy told Stormy to stay and ran for the wreck. She crouched down and looked inside. Ripley sat blindfolded and trembling. Her hands were still bound and her body was scratched from the crash.

"Ripley," she said gently. "It's me, Poppy. You're safe. Now let me take your blindfold off and help you out."

She helped ease the blindfold off, thankful to see her eyes were open and showed no sign of head trauma. Poppy then cut her bonds and cautiously helped her climb from the car, thankful there were no major signs of injury. Ripley stepped out of the car and stood on shaky legs.

Poppy glanced back at where Lex had Kevin down on the ground. Kevin was swearing, thrashing and trying in vain to strike out against Lex. But in an instant, he had him pinned. Then Lex flipped the perp over onto his stomach and tied his hands behind his back with a zip tie.

No sooner had Ripley stepped free from the wreckage than her eyes rose toward the air hangar. "Nolan!"

"Ripley!" Nolan called. Her brother stumbled toward her with what looked like the bandanna Poppy had been blindfolded with tied over the bullet wound. "I'm sorry! I'm so, so sorry!"

She stood back and let the siblings run across the tarmac to each other. Lex marched Kevin over to her. He'd muffled the man's swear words with a gag. Poppy opened the back door of Lex's truck, called Stormy to get out and watched as Lex pushed Kevin inside and locked the door.

Then she turned toward the private plane with the captured bear cubs inside with Lex on her one side and Stormy at the other.

"We need to stop the plane," she said, even as she felt the futility of their situation wash over her. "We can't let them take the bear cubs."

But it was too late. Already they could see the small jet had turned around. Its propellers whirled and flaps rose. She watched as it taxied down the runway ready to lift off.

Her heart sank and her footsteps stopped. She felt Lex grab her hand and squeeze it tightly. She squeezed it back as tears filled her eyes. The plane was leaving. They'd lost. The bears were being flown off by an unscrupulous criminal and there was nothing they could do about it.

Then a loud crash and terrifying growl filled the air, as the brown bear broke through its cage.

FOURTEEN

Poppy watched as the expensive jet swerved suddenly, trying to avoid the brown bear as it charged. The plane spun wildly, spinning off the runway like a toy top out of control. It smashed into a tree with a deafening crunch, snapping off a wing.

She gasped a breath. The bear turned and lumbered back into the woods. Then she felt Lex tug her fingers, and they ran together across the tarmac to the wrecked aircraft, with Stormy by their side.

The cockpit door flew open.

"Freeze!" Poppy shouted to the two men inside. She raised her badge and weapon. "I'm Trooper Poppy Walsh and you're under arrest."

Beside her Lex was yanking open the back of the plane. Two small bear cubs looked up at him from inside dog crates.

"It's okay, guys," Lex told the frightened cubs softly. "We've got you. You're safe now."

The client, pilot and Kevin were all sitting handcuffed in one end of the airplane hangar, while Nolan and Ripley sat huddled in the other end what felt like moments later, when she saw three rescue helicopters hovering above them. Will leaped out of the first one as it landed, followed by troopers from the Juneau unit. And suddenly, activity was everywhere as she briefed the team, oversaw the arrests and made sure Nolan and Ripley got medical attention before they were placed into custody. The siblings were already pledging to tell law enforcement everything as their statements were being taken. In the midst of all this, Poppy saw Lex signal her to join him away from the crowd.

She walked over.

"I've got to go coordinate with the animal rescue wildlife center about taking the bear cubs," Lex said. "I'm very hopeful they'll be able to be rehabilitated and released back into the wild. But I didn't want to leave without saying goodbye and telling you that everyone's invited back to our place for food later tonight when this wraps up."

She looked around at the crew of law enforcement and medical professionals expertly wrapping up the scene. "I'm sure everyone will appreciate that."

"You okay?" Lex asked. "You seem a bit down when I'd have thought you should be celebrating."

Was she that transparent around him?

"Do you think the brown bear that charged the plane will be okay?" she asked.

"I hope so," Lex said. "But I'll make sure the park rangers try to locate it." Then he frowned. "I just wish we'd been able to save the mama blue bear. It honestly hurts my heart to know that although we saved those little cubs, they're orphans now."

Unexpected tears brushed her eyelids.

"Me, too," she said.

"I think I'm learning that just because an ending doesn't look the way I hoped it would doesn't mean it's not a happy one." His arm slipped around her shoulders and he pulled her closer to his side in a half hug. "Will I see you back at the house later?"

"I'll be there," she whispered.

He walked away.

But will my own story have a happy ending?

Night had just begun to fall by the time she finally made it back to the bed-and-breakfast. The cozy living space seemed filled to the brim with happy people, including troopers, rescue workers, park rangers and what seemed like the entire town's worth of friends and neighbors. Potluck dishes spilled over every surface. Will had set up a laptop on the mantel and opened a video chat link for the K-9 team so any of them who wanted to pop into the celebration could. Poppy had made small talk, double-checked that Stormy was happily curled up on the floor with Danny and Mushroom, under Gillian's watchful eye, and somehow managed to avoid ever being completely alone with Lex before she flew out with Will later tonight.

She slipped out the sliding glass door and into the backyard, craving a moment alone with her thoughts before she had to pack up and say goodbye. Poppy watched as the sun dipped slowly behind the distant mountains, casting the glaciers in dusty rose and purple hues.

Help my heart, Lord. It feels like You just brought Lex back into my life and now we're going our separate ways again.

She heard the sliding door open behind her and the gentle babble of voices inside the house grew louder for a moment, before it closed again. Then she heard the footsteps of someone walking across the porch, coming down the steps and crossing the grass toward her. Somehow she knew it was Lex, even before she heard him say her name.

"Poppy?" His voice was soft and husky.

She turned around and there he was standing behind her. The dying light cast long shadows down his handsome face. But it was the depth of emotion pooling in his dark brown eyes that made her heartbeat catch in her chest and everything inside her long to throw her arms around his neck and pull him close.

Help me, Lord. How do I say goodbye?

"How's it going?" she asked.

"Pretty good," Lex said. "I have been wondering something, though, and I didn't know how to ask it." He ran his hand over the back of his neck. "At the airfield, when Kevin crashed the truck, you ran for Ripley and I took him down. Was that for operational reasons or because you knew, on some level, I wanted to be the one who took down the guy who killed my friend?"

"Probably a bit of both," Poppy admitted. "As a trooper my top responsibility in that moment was making sure Ripley was okay.

But I'm glad you were there to take Kevin down. Two things can be true at once. I've gotten a lot better at thinking I have to do everything by myself. And I think we make a good team."

"So do I," Lex admitted gruffly.

Poppy felt a tired smile cross her face She glanced at Lex and saw a nervous grin brush his lips, too. Then he took a deep breath.

"Which is why I'd like to fly back to Anchorage with you tonight," he said. "Partly because I want to visit Johnny's family to pay my respects and ask if there's anything I can do to help them with the funeral. Also, I've been talking to people I know at the animal rescue sanctuary where the baby blue bear cubs are headed and wanted to see what I could do to help the little guys heal from their adventure and start a new life in the wild. Turns out, they're hiring and want to talk to me about a potential job. As much as I've enjoyed living here, I think it's time for a new adventure." He took her hands and linked his fingers through hers. "And I want you to be a big part of it. If you want to be."

She felt her breath catch. He brought her hands to his lips and brushed a kiss over her knuckles.

"What are you saying, Lex?" she asked.

"That I'm a better man with you than I am alone," Lex said. "You strengthen me and push me, Poppy. You're strong in areas I'm weak and bring out the best in who I want to be. Moving with my mom and Danny back to Anchorage and starting a new life will be challenging. And I don't want to do it without you. In fact, I don't ever want to do anything big without you ever again."

"I don't want to do anything big without you ever again, either," she confessed.

He pulled his hands from hers and wrapped them around her waist as her fingers slid up and linked behind his neck.

"I'm in love with you, Poppy," Lex said. "Head over heels. I always have been. My mother thinks you're amazing and Danny adores having you and Stormy around. You complete my family in a way nobody could."

She felt happy tears shine in her eyes. "I love you, too. I never stopped."

"I'm so glad to hear that," Lex said, and his grin grew wider than she'd ever seen before. "Because I want to marry you. I want to be your husband and I want you to be my wife and Danny's mom. But more than that, I want to help you plan our new life together.

The boring bank meetings, the budgets, the chores—I'm here for all of it."

"I want to marry you, too."

Then his lips met hers for a long moment and he kissed her, lifting her feet up off the ground as he swept her into his embrace. And as the sunset swept the Alaskan sky, Poppy wrapped her arms tightly around the man she knew without a shadow of a doubt that she was going to love forever.

* * * * *

*Look for the next book in the Alaska K-9
Unit series,* Undercover Mission
by Sharon Dunn,
available in June 2021.

ALASKA K-9 UNIT
*These state troopers fight for justice with
the help of their brave canine partners.*

Dear Reader,

I ended up moving unexpectedly while finishing this book and, because I was rushing, accidentally hurt myself and ended up going to the hospital.

"Don't use your hand for at least a week," the doctor told me kindly and firmly. "We don't want you needing to come back because you busted your stitches."

"Absolutely," I said. "Got it!"

Then I promptly tried to unpack and move furniture one-handed.

"You haven't washed your hair in a while," a friend pointed out after a few days. Despite the fact I'd turned down their offer to pick up groceries for me they'd still baked me a chocolate loaf. "Do you need help? I could wash and brush your hair for you."

"Oh, no, I'm fine!" I said, telling them I'd just wrap some plastic bags around my hand.

It wasn't until my lovely agent, Melissa, finally called and told me, "You know, we still love you even when you're hurt!" that I realized just how hard I'd been trying to do it all on my own.

So, I'm dedicating this book to all of you

who, like me, find it hard to ask for help and to all of you who've been reaching out to those in need. I hope this Alaskan K-9 series helps you find a bit of joy, fun and an escape from the stresses of everyday life. I'm looking forward to reading them all!

Thank you as always for sharing this journey with me,
Maggie